granuaile

The Pirate Queen

The story of the
sixteenth-century
she-king of Connacht,
a leader of men and the
terror of the western seas.

A real-life adventure

Morgan Llywelyn

Morgan Llywelyn lives in Dublin. She has written
numerous international bestselling historical
novels, such as *Lion of Ireland*, *The Horse
Goddess*, *Bard*, *Grania* and *On Raven's Wing*.
Her first books for children, *Brian Ború* and
Strongbow, both won Bisto awards.

GRANUAILE

Morgan Llywelyn

THE O'BRIEN PRESS
DUBLIN

First published 2001 by The O'Brien Press Ltd.
20 Victoria Road, Dublin 6, Ireland.
Tel. +353 1 4923333; Fax. +353 1 4922777
E-mail: books@obrien.ie
Website: www.obrien.ie

ISBN: 0-86278-578-2

British Library Cataloguing-in-publication Data
A catalogue record for this title is available
from the British Library

1 2 3 4 5 6 7 8 9 10
01 02 03 04 05 06 07 08 09

The O'Brien Press receives
assistance from

the arts
council
an chomhairle
ealaíon
50+

Layout and design: The O'Brien Press Ltd.
Colour separations: C&A Print Services Ltd., Dublin
Printing: Cox & Wyman Ltd.

contents

PROLOGUE 7

1 THE PIRATE QUEEN 10

2 ROCKFLEET 16

3 THE CALL OF THE SEA 23

4 THE QUEEN ACROSS THE SEA 27

5 REBELLION IN IAR CONNACHT 29

6 CHRISTMAS AT BELCLARE 34

7 BESIEGED 39

8 RELIGIOUS PERSECUTION 41

9 DONAL O'FLAHERTY 44

10 HOMECOMING 50

11 A PIRATE AT WORK 57

12 THE LONG ARM OF ELIZABETH 60

13 KIDNAP 62

14 NEGOTIATING WITH THE ENEMY 65

15 A BOLD PLAN 68

16 ATTACKING THE GREAT EARL 71

17 LIMERICK GAOL 73

18 THE WEIGHT OF FEAR 78

19 DUBLIN CASTLE 80

20 WINNING THE GAME 86

21 BACK TO WAR 90

22 THE PRINCES OF THE NORTH 95

23 THE DEATH OF RICHARD-IN-IRON 98

24 STEALING TIBBOTT 102

25 SUMMONED 106

26 THE DEVIL'S HOOK 109

27 FEEDING THE ENEMY 114

28 PLOTS AND PLANS 117

29 THE CAPTURE OF RED HUGH 122

30 A PARDON FROM PERROT 126

31 THE SPANISH ARMADA 128

32 NURSE TO ALL REBELLIONS 134

33 THE HOUND'S JAWS 139

34 ESCAPE! 141

35 BINGHAM STRIKES 144

36 ELIZABETH 146

37 HOME IN TRIUMPH 150

38 TURNING AGAINST O'DONNELL 153

39 THE WIND HAS CHANGED 155

EPILOGUE 157

prologue

June, the Year of Our Lord 1567,
somewhere off the south coast of Ireland

My Little Son,

Three days ago you entered my life. You are a special gift from God when I had thought myself long past having children. Your name is to be Tibbott-ne-Long, Tibbott of the Long Ships. But I shall call you Toby. Toby will be a secret name between us.

Words do not come easily to me. My life has been one of action rather than talk. When you are older you will want to know about your mother. Wild stories are told of me and you will need to have the truth. I may not be able to tell you myself. Life is uncertain. So I have decided to write letters that will speak for me some day. As the daughter of an Irish chieftain I was taught to read and write.

Your father is descended from the Normans, and like most of his people, he can neither read nor write. But you will. I shall insist upon it. And I will see that my letters are saved for you to read.

While I pen these words you are sleeping nearby. You are gently swaying in the little hammock my men constructed of fishing net and hung from the ceiling beams of my cabin. How peaceful you look, how untroubled. Pray God your life might always be so. But I fear that it will not. As we begin, so we continue.

We are aboard a ship of my fleet off the southwest coast of Ireland. I frequently sail these waters in a fine caravel built in Spain to my order. Trade is my business and that of the men I lead. We are oft times accused of piracy, but that is not strictly true. We simply use the sea and those who travel upon it in order to support ourselves. The day after you were born we were attacked at sea by real pirates. They were Turks who roam these waters in their corsairs looking for victims.

I refuse to be anyone's victim.

When one of my men came below to tell me that the battle was going against us, I sprang from my bunk. I was still weak from bringing you into the world, but I seized a blunderbuss and went storming up on deck with my hair unbound and my clothes undone.

When the pirates saw me they were truly frightened. I must have looked a wild woman indeed, waving a gun around and screaming at them in fury. My men took heart from my courage, and together we defeated the enemy and captured their ship. How I laughed!

Laden with plunder taken from the plunderers, we set sail for home. We shall enter Clew Bay with the sunset.

You are to be Toby, but what shall you call me? I am known by many names – ship's captain, she-king of the western seas, pirate. But whatever men say about me, I shall remain your loving mother.

Always,
Granuaile

chapter one

the pirate queen

The vast expanse of Clew Bay mirrors the heavens above. Freckled with countless tiny islands, the bay is embraced by mountains. To the north are Slieve Mór and the Nephin Beg range. The western rampart is Cnoc Mór on Clare Island. On the south side of the bay rises the most magnificent of them all – Patrick's holy mountain, the great quartzite cone of Croagh Patrick.

This part of Connacht is known as Umhall Uí Mháille, the Territory of the O'Malleys. As Granuaile's fleet nears Clew Bay, huge flocks of kittiwakes and fulmars are winging toward Clare Island for the night. The birds' harsh cries mingle with the welcoming shouts of the islanders. Men and women run along the headland to wave to the approaching ships.

Standing tall in the prow of her flagship galley, Granuaile waves in return.

The island's lookout lights a fire to signal the return of the fleet, and answering fires begin to bloom all around the bay. There is an air of celebration. Granuaile's arrival means another successful trading voyage – or perhaps plunder to share. She never comes home empty-handed. For generations the O'Malleys have demanded a fee from any merchant ships that enter their territorial waters. If the captains refuse to pay, their vessels are boarded and their cargo seized.

Most of the fleet will offload at Clare Island. Granuaile's flagship and two other galleys sail on across the bay toward Belclare. Dun Béal an Chláir – the Fort at the Mouth of the Plain – is her father's stronghold. She always takes the choicest goods to him.

The wind has died with the setting sun. Granuaile orders her crews to lower the sails. The men take to their oars, and soon the galleys are skimming forward again.

Long snakes of torchlight wind their way over wooded hills and across grassy meadows. Her people are hurrying to welcome Granuaile home. Her caravel, flying the flag of the white seahorse, is the first to reach the shore. Water hisses and foams on the shingle beach. Crew members call to their waiting families, then vault over the side and come running ashore.

A man on a lathered horse approaches at a thundering gallop. People jump out of his way. He dismounts and waits, as his horse paws at the ground. His pride demands that Granuaile come to him.

He is watching for the tall, strongly built ship's captain with her weather-beaten complexion and mane of heavy, black hair. On shipboard she dresses like a man, in close-fitting woollen trews and a linen shirt. Her feet are bare to give her a grip on slippery wooden decks. Some might mistake her for a sailor. But when he sees her wading through the surf, Richard Bourke recognises Granuaile immediately. Even knee-deep in foaming water, she carries herself like a queen.

In her arms is a bundle wrapped in a seaman's shirt. As she approaches Richard, the bundle gives a loud cry and waves a tiny fist in the air. Granuaile laughs.

'What is that?' Richard demands to know.

She opens her eyes very wide, looking innocent. 'An infant. Have you never seen one before?'

'I have of course, but where did it come from?'

She waves a casual hand toward her caravel. 'My ship.'

He is trying hard not to lose his temper. He has learned that it is dangerous to lose one's temper with Granuaile – she fights back. 'How did an infant come to be on the ship?' he wants to know.

'Simple enough. I gave birth to him.'

Richard stares at her. 'You?'

'That is what I said.'

He can no longer contain his rage. 'You did not tell me you were expecting a child! You went off to sea where anything might have happened to my son and you did not even tell me! Were you keeping him a secret in order to deceive me?'

Granuaile gives him another innocent stare. 'Did I say this baby is a boy?'

Richard makes a grab for the child. She swings away, easily keeping the infant out of his reach. She is as tall as

Richard and nearly as strong, and her eyes flame with defiance. 'Do not try to seize what is mine!' she says in a ringing voice. 'I remind you that we are divorced.'

Richard is her second husband. They had been married less than a year when Granuaile learned that she was with child. Richard was away at the time. He had left her at Rockfleet Castle while he went to take part in one of the border disputes that were part of Irish life. Already Granuaile had feared the marriage was a mistake. My second mistake, she thought sadly. But this time I am wiser than I was when I wed Donal O'Flaherty.

If Richard came back and found that a child was on the way, he would refuse to let her go to sea any more. He would insist she become a traditional wife, meekly submitting to her husband's wishes, with no life of her own.

But Granuaile had tasted another life. She did not intend to give it up.

When Richard returned she had gone out onto the ramparts of the castle, staying behind the stone parapet so he could not see the thickening of her body. She cupped her hands around her mouth and shouted down to her husband, 'Richard Bourke, I dismiss you!'

Sitting on his horse, tired and dirty, expecting a hot meal and a comfortable bed, he had stared up at his wife with his mouth hanging open.

'You what?!'

'I dismiss you, Richard,' Granuaile had repeated, keeping her voice calm. She must be in control, as she was aboard ship. 'Under Brehon Law I claim this castle as my marriage portion. You have other strongholds, make one of them your home.'

Brehon Law had governed the Gael long before the coming of Saint Patrick. Although the Irish had converted to Christianity a thousand years before, they continued to respect the old ways. In the wilds of Connacht the Gaelic laws still ruled. Rather than risk an outright confrontation on the issue, the Church turned a blind eye.

At Granuaile's request, she and Richard had been married in the Gaelic style. Brehon Law allowed a woman to own property in her own right. It also permitted a marriage 'for one year certain', to give people a chance to decide if they were suited. At the end of that year either party could end the marriage, simply by saying 'I dismiss you'. The wife could then take back her dowry. Instead of the dowry, Granuaile was claiming Rockfleet, an exceptionally secure stronghold on the north shore of Clew Bay.

Because she and Richard were both Catholics, they had also been married by a priest. The Catholic Church did not recognise divorce. Therefore Granuaile was not really ending the marriage; she was simply informing Richard that he no longer had any control over her. To make her point she had barred the castle's only door against him. A number of her men, well armed, stood guard.

Richard had stared up at her for a long time. Then he rode his horse around the castle, muttering to himself. He dismounted and pounded on the heavy oak door. He made threats.

Granuaile had ignored him.

Finally he got back on his horse.

When she was satisfied that Richard was on his way to his other castle at Burrishoole, Granuaile went to join her fleet. There was work to be done. Clan O'Malley depended on her for support and her first obligation was to them.

Carrying her child under her heart, Granuaile had gone back to sea.

chapter two

ROCKFLEET

When Granuaile returns to Clew Bay with her infant son, she allows Richard Bourke to accompany them to Rockfleet. She gives orders that he is to be treated like a guest, however, rather than lord of the castle.

Richard is not happy about the arrangement. He stalks through the chambers, growling at his wife and bellowing at the servants.

A traditional Norman castle is a vast structure, capable of sheltering scores of nobles and their retainers. Rockfleet Castle is much smaller, a typical, square-shaped stone tower house occupied by one family. It stands at the head of an inlet that opens into Clew Bay. At high tide water laps the foot of the tower. At low tide the lawn is seaweed.

Dark and forbidding, Rockfleet defies both man and the elements. Two corner turrets rise above the parapet on opposite sides. Loopholes, through which guns can be fired, overlook the approaches. High up on the east wall is a peculiar, arched doorway that gives on to empty space.

There is a fifty-foot drop to the rocks below. Using this loading bay, goods are delivered to the top of the castle by means of a pulley.

Rockfleet is guarded by, and supplied from, the sea.

The tower comprises four storeys, with an armoury at ground level. Kitchens and a rectangular banqueting hall made of timber and thatch stand a little distance away. If they catch fire, as they frequently do, they can burn without endangering the main structure.

Within the tower, a spiral stone staircase leads to the great hall at the top. This is the main living area. The bedchamber is one storey below. Opening off the stairs between the two levels is a tiny garderobe, or indoor privy. The waste pipe runs down through the wall to the foot of the tower. The turn of the tide flushes it clean.

Through the garderobe window one can see Croagh Patrick.

Even in summer, a fire is kept burning in the massive arched fireplace in the great hall. Each storey has its own fireplace. From the outside the tower house looks cold and bleak, but the stone walls absorb the heat and radiate it back into the rooms. When every fireplace is alight at once the building can become too hot for comfort.

The floor of the great hall is made of coloured flagstones. Smoke has stained the painted leather wall hangings, darkening their bright colours. An oaken table in the centre of the room holds an assortment of tankards and several fine silver goblets. A pair of large, shaggy hounds sprawl beneath the table. Bits of armour and weapons are scattered about the room, as are baskets and a fishing net.

Beside the hearth, Granuaile lounges on a bench padded with sheepskin. She is nursing her little son and pretending to ignore her husband.

'You barred me from my own castle and hid the fact of my son from me!' Richard accuses, slamming his fist on the table. 'Worse yet, you plotted to deceive me while I was away fighting for your benefit.'

'I acted within the law, there was no deception,' Granuaile drawls. 'Nor were you acting for my benefit.' She turns her gaze toward the flames. The firelight is reflected in her dark eyes. 'I did not ask you to go floundering around in the rain trying to capture a bog for me, Richard.'

'Not just a bog, but some good pasture land. I have to enlarge our holdings. I need power, and land is power. Even more than that, I need gold to give to my followers. Without a band of my own warriors how can I ever hope to become The MacWilliam?'

'That title means nothing to me.' Bending her head, Granuaile presses her chapped lips to the top of her baby's downy skull.

Richard says, 'The MacWilliam is chief of all the Bourkes of Mayo.'

'I am leader of the O'Malleys of Mayo,' she counters.

'But you have no title. A woman cannot be elected to a chieftainship.'

'I rule my people by land and sea,' she reminds him. 'What else would you call me?'

'What some call you behind your back,' he says with a snort. 'She-king.'

He means it to be an insult, but she is not insulted. Lifting her chin, she stares at him from beneath level brows. 'I am,' says Granuaile. 'I *am* a she-king.'

Richard is known as Richard-in-Iron, leader of the Bourkes of Carra, a branch of the large Bourke tribe. The Bourkes were originally called de Burgo. They are descended from Normans who came to Ireland from England three hundred years earlier in the service of an English king. Once they arrived, they liked Ireland so much that they decided to stay.

The land the Bourkes occupy used to be part of O'Malley territory. The O'Malleys did not offer the new-comers much opposition when they first settled on the north shore of Clew Bay. The natives thought there was room enough for a few strangers. Little did they realise that these Normans were but the thin edge of the wedge.

The Normans married Irish women and adopted Irish customs. Yet in some ways they remained like the English who had sent them. More than once, Granuaile had said to her husband, 'Your kind will never have enough until they have everything.'

Richard sees her baby only as someone to carry on his name and increase his holdings. To Granuaile, Toby is small and vulnerable and dear, an individual in his own right. She will never allow Richard to have control of her son. Nor is she willing to give her husband the profits from her seafaring. That is the real reason behind the quarrel between them now.

While he blusters and threatens, she holds her baby and waits for the storm to blow over. Others know Richard as a violent man. He has only once tried to use force on Granuaile. On that occasion she hit him in the belly with her doubled fist, hard enough to knock the wind from him. She does not think he will hit her again. But if he does, she is ready.

Granuaile is always ready. On ship or on land, she carries a knife in her belt.

'You do not sail the seas, Richard,' she says to him when he finally stops shouting and slumps onto a bench. 'I do. You do not take the risks. I do. The fleet enables me to support my clan as my father did before me. As a chieftain yourself, surely you understand that is my first duty.'

Granuaile's father is Dubhdara Ua Máille, The Black Oak of the O'Malleys. He is the chief of the clan. Over the years Dubhdara built up a sea trade extending from Scotland and the North Sea to Spain and Portugal. The Black Oak has only one son, Donal of the Pipes. His mother is not Dubhdara's wife, however. Besides, Donal has no stomach for the sea. So when Dubhdara grew old, Granuaile took over the O'Malley fleet.

Being a sea captain is a singular occupation for an Irish woman. Some people are shocked, but her clan is very proud of her. She has even extended the trade routes.

She is not about to give her hard-won profits to Richard Bourke to pay for petty squabbles with his kinsmen!

Warfare is the normal condition in Connacht, as it is throughout Ireland. Gaelic clans have always fought over cattle. Gaelic chieftains have always fought to extend their territory. The Normans have readily adopted this way of life because they first came into Ireland as mercenaries themselves.

Yet in spite of constant conflict, Ireland in the sixteenth century is prosperous. Much of the island is covered with great forests of timber. Well-watered grasslands support large herds of cattle. The woods teem with game and the lakes and rivers are full of fish. The Gaelic nobility wear masses of gold jewellery, and even their servants possess ornaments of bronze and iron. People of all classes dine on beef and bacon and buttermilk. The Gael have dominated this land for two thousand years. It is hard to imagine anything changing.

Yet change is coming.

Since the twelfth century, the English have sought without success to conquer Ireland. The Norman mercenaries they have sent have been absorbed into the country. The Anglo-Normans have become, some say, more Irish than the Irish themselves. Now they are called the 'Old English', because a new wave of would-be conquerors has arrived from England.

Elizabeth Tudor, Queen of England, has sent shiploads of warriors and administrators to carve up Ireland. They are known as the 'New English'. They have no desire to become Irish, and have merely come to plunder the country for their monarch. Meanwhile, in foreign seaports, Granuaile has heard tales of a New World beyond the western ocean. The English ruler hopes to seize this New World as well. There is no limit to her greed, it seems.

As Granuaile hugs her small son to her breast, she thinks about that other she-king across the Irish Sea. She feels a chill run up her spine. If Elizabeth succeeds in her dreams of conquest, what effect will that have on Toby's life? On his childhood?

It is less disturbing for Granuaile to recall her own childhood. Gratefully she looks back to the days when she was wild and free.

chapter three
the call of the sea

When Granuaile was a child, Clare Island was her summer home. In her memories of that distant, happy time, the sun shone every day. She was never hungry or thirsty or frightened. Each day was an adventure.

In the summer her family went booleying, taking their cattle to the upland pastures to graze. They made huts of wattle and thatch that only lasted for the season. Mostly they lived under the open sky. Granuaile loved the sky at night above Clare Island. Lying on her back in the fragrant grass, she would listen as Dubhdara taught her the names of the stars.

Cattle were important, providing leather, meat, milk and butter, but the sea was their main source of income. The O'Malley fleet travelled great distances, trading salted and pickled fish, surplus hides and tallow, for casks of wine and ingots of copper. Through the vast network of sea trade they also obtained figs and pomegranates and silk, cumin and cinnamon and saffron. Clew Bay was the home port for these enterprises.

Granuaile had made her first voyage from the dock below the tower house on Clare Island. 'Stay away from the shore, the sea is not safe for children,' Margaret, her mother, had often said. But Granuaile was enchanted by the shining, leaping waves, with their crests of white foam. One day she persuaded Dubhdara to take her as far as Achill Island in his boat. The sea was rough but the little girl was not seasick. Her father was very proud. When they returned home, he laughed at his wife's fears. 'My daughter is an O'Malley,' he said. 'She's a born sea-horse!'

As a reward, Dubhdara gave Granuaile a coracle of her own – a small, round boat made of hide stretched over a wooden frame. She could paddle herself around in the shallows, and for a time she was satisfied. But not for long. The open sea beckoned to her, a great blue kingdom stretching from sunrise to sunset!

Granuaile's next boat was a currach – a long, narrow fishing boat, sealed with pitch to keep the water out. Her father's sailors did the rowing while she rode in the prow, gliding back and forth among the islands that dotted the bay. She liked to pretend that she was a white seahorse. Or a ship's captain, like her father. Giving orders. Going to exotic places.

Dubhdara captained the O'Malley fleet on long trading voyages. Some leaders are cruel to their men, but Granuaile's father always believed that praise wins more than punishment. The men and young lads who sailed with him adored him. When they came home they told wonderful stories of their adventures in faraway lands.

Granuaile listened eagerly to their tales. 'Having to stay home with the women is worse than being in a prison,' she complained.

'But you are a woman, or soon will be,' insisted her mother. She dressed Granuaile's hair in curls and plaits and made her wear petticoats that were always getting in the way. Margaret did everything she could to keep her daughter from going out in a boat. 'I am always afraid something will happen,' she said.

'Nothing is happening!' Granuaile would argue. 'Nothing! I am getting older and older and everything around me is staying just the same.'

One fine spring morning in her eleventh year, the girl cut off her long hair and disguised herself as a boy. She sneaked on board her father's largest trading galley and hid in the cargo hold. She would never forget the way cold water sloshed around her ankles, or the ancient smell of fish that clung to the timbers. Listening to the hiss of water beneath the vessel, she waited for the hours to pass. At last she fell asleep. She woke up chilled and stiff, but at sea. At sea!

When she was sure they had travelled too far to turn back, she went up on deck.

At first Dubhdara was angry, or pretended to be. He started to scold her, then began to laugh instead. His laughter was a great, happy roar, like a huge wave breaking. Granuaile rode on the crest of that wave, knowing that everything would be all right. The Black Oak could never remain angry with his daughter for very long. She was too much like him.

After that she went on every voyage and learned to handle every type of ship. 'If God does not give me a suitable son, at least he has given me Granuaile,' Dubhdara is given to say. 'There is no sailor her equal on Clew Bay.'

chapter four

the queen across the sea

September, the Year of Our Lord 1569, Rockfleet

My dear son,

I am sending you away to be fostered. You are too young to understand, but this is an ancient custom in Ireland. Fosterage creates strong ties between the clan of the original parents and that of the foster parents. Many useful alliances are forged in this way.

I would have preferred to keep you with me. You are the last babe I shall ever have. But I must think of your future.

There is a powerful woman across the Irish Sea whom I have never met. She does not know me, yet I can sense Elizabeth Tudor lurking like a great black spider high up in the corner of a room. Three years ago she sent one of her men, Henry Sidney, to Connacht, seeking submission to the English Crown. He offered the chieftains bribes, which he called rewards.

On behalf of Clan O'Malley, Dubhdara proudly refused. However, The MacWilliam, chieftain of all the Bourkes of Mayo, submitted. He swore loyalty to the English queen in return for gifts and a promise of peace between his people and hers. The MacWilliam swore his oath in Latin rather than in English. We all know Latin thanks to the Church, and for the sake of trade I also speak Spanish. Very few in Connacht have any English. It is a coarse, crude language, without music. I would not cripple my tongue with it.

After Sidney departed, the chieftains forgot about their promises. I could have told him they would. In Ireland pledges are often given between provincial kings and clan chieftains, and they are just as often broken. But Sidney will return. Sooner rather than later, he will return, and with an army at his back. Knowing that surely, I am trying to plan for the future.

I have decided to have you fostered by another of the Bourke families. Elizabeth's men seem more tolerant of the Anglo-Normans than they are of the Irish. The day may come when you are thankful to have such connections.

As for me, I remain Gaelic in my heart and soul.

Always,
Granuaile

chapter five

Rebellion in Iar Connacht

With a heavy heart, Granuaile sends her two-year-old son to live with Edmund MacTibbott at Castleaffey, south of Burrishoole. She vows to visit him whenever time allows, but the fleet has first claim on her. The bay is teeming with herring, and the O'Malleys are fishermen.

There are larger fish out in the ocean – fish with no fins or gills, yet they are valuable prey. Granuaile conceals her swiftest galleys among the many islands in Clew Bay. When foreign cargo ships sail past the mouth of the bay, they dart out and attack. Granuaile demands that merchants pay licences for using her waters. If they refuse, she seizes their goods.

For this the English accuse her of piracy. The accusation makes her laugh. 'Elizabeth Tudor's seamen are all pirates,' Granuaile points out to Richard Bourke. 'That is how the English she-king increases her wealth. The one called Walter Raleigh is the most famous pirate of them all, and a great favourite of hers, I understand. I suppose she is fond of him in the same way that I am fond of the

29

brave men who follow me.' She cannot resist boasting, 'My men know I care about them, that is why they will never desert me.'

'Do not be so sure,' Richard responds glumly. 'One cannot be certain of anything in this world. I thought my wife would be loyal to me, yet you give your loyalty to the O'Malleys.'

'I give my loyalty to all who depend upon me,' she replies. 'It is not my fault there are so many of them.'

Even though Toby is now being fostered, he still depends on her. She can feel him as if they are attached by an invisible silver cord. 'Oh, my little son,' she cries out to him silently, in the dark of the night. She likes to imagine that her call spans the miles. She sends him little gifts from her voyages, and loving letters.

The stronghold of Castleaffey houses the large family of Edmund MacTibbott, who is fostering several children in addition to his own. A foster parent must provide at least as well for his fosterlings as he does for children of his own blood. As they grow, the boys will learn the skills of javelin, sword, dagger and dart, as well as horse riding and the use of firearms. Granuaile has begun importing matchlock guns and wheel-lock pistols into Mayo.

Because the Anglo-Normans, like the Irish, are Catholic, a monk from Burrishoole Abbey gives the children religious instruction. He also carries letters to Tibbott from his mother. Granuaile has asked that the letters be read aloud to her son. The child listens with wide eyes. Even though he does not yet understand all the words, he knows they come to him warm with his mother's breath.

There are ever more English vessels in the waters off Connacht. Granuaile imagines that she can feel Elizabeth's breath on the back of her neck. The English she-king resents every bit of cargo, every gold coin that is seized around Clew Bay. Elizabeth plans to convict Granuaile of piracy and put her in prison. No one has actually said this yet, but Granuaile knows. She knows it as she knows when rain is coming.

In February 1570, she has Tibbott transferred to another foster parent, Myles MacEvilly of Kinturk Castle. Kinturk is a sturdy castle, farther inland. Safer. There Tibbott learns to read. Granuaile's letters are sealed with red wax bearing the imprint of three seahorses. The boy's first attempts at writing are his replies. His mother saves them in a small silver casket which she always keeps with her, even when she is at sea. Sometimes when Granuaile is alone, she takes out the letters and reads them one by one, smiling at the childish scrawl. When she smiles her stern face softens and there is a warm light in her dark eyes.

Her fears for the future are not without reason.

Elizabeth's officials undertake a survey of the entire province of Connacht and divided it into 'baronies'. They list the clans and chieftains of every barony, including Mayo. This is done to help them set up an English government in the territory. The Bourkes of Carra, Richard's family, resent this imposed foreign authority as much as the native Irish do.

When they learn that some of the O'Flaherty clan are rebelling in Iar Connacht, Richard wants to go south and join them. He persuades Granuaile to give him enough gold to finance an assault on an English garrison beyond Galway. 'Be loyal to me for once!' he argues. She can hardly refuse. With a fresh supply of weaponry, Richard and his men march off to war.

Unfortunately they find themselves on the other side of the battle from the old MacWilliam, chief of the entire Bourke clan in Mayo. Because of his submission to the Crown, The MacWilliam stands with Elizabeth's supporters.

At Rockfleet, Granuaile waits tensely to hear the outcome. In her mind she is already framing a letter to Toby, telling him of victory over the foreigners.

On land messages are shouted from hilltop to hilltop, from man to man, in the old Gaelic way. In one day news of a battle can travel halfway across Ireland. But the news, when it comes, is not good.

The battle in which Richard took part has settled nothing. As often happens, both sides claim victory. He returns to Rockfleet to lick his wounds. 'You have wasted arms and men and what do you have to show for it?' Granuaile demands to know. But she gives him a hot meal and hospitality. Any defiance of the English pleases her.

Unfortunately, the battle has left the large Bourke tribe badly split, between support for, and opposition to, the English Crown. When the old MacWilliam dies shortly afterward, Richard expects to become the new chieftain. 'I proved myself by being willing to fight the English,' he reminds his kinsmen.

The Bourkes elect a man called Shane MacOliverus instead. He has a reputation for being lavish with his hospitality, even more lavish than he can afford. He also is a man who will do almost anything for a quiet life.

Although Shane MacOliverus names Richard as his *tanaiste*, his chosen successor, that is small comfort. Richard is furious. In his own mind, he had already become The MacWilliam. Once more he stalks through Rockfleet, muttering and slamming his fist against the furniture.

Granuaile observes, 'I think the Bourkes are frightened of Elizabeth, Richard. So they have elected a chieftain with a peaceful nature, one who has not made English enemies.'

'It is no comfort to think of my kinsmen as cowards,' Richard growls.

'Be patient. Shane MacOliverus will not live forever. Power shifts and shifts again. Sometimes it seems like one great game, like the chess I used to play with my father in the hall at Belclare. Men move here and there, words are spoken, threats are made. Strategy is everything. Listen to the advice I give you and bide your time.'

christmas at belclare

'You only married me to get your hands on Rockfleet Castle!' Richard shouts during one of their frequent rows.

Granuaile laughs. 'You forget that I have strongholds all around Clew Bay, and even a castle in Iar Connacht which I won for myself with a sword in my hand. I would hardly have married you for another set of walls and a roof.'

'Then why did you?'

She shrugs. 'I no longer remember. Because both our families wanted it, I suppose.' She is genuinely fond of Richard Bourke, a handsome man with dark auburn hair and bright blue eyes, but she will never admit this. He is certainly a more satisfactory husband than her first one was. But Richard now lives elsewhere and visits only at her invitation.

Richard tolerates the situation because Granuaile is a valuable asset. A wealthy wife is highly prized by the Anglo-Normans. Granuaile even has the ability to increase her wealth through her own actions. Unfortunately she is a difficult woman. Her gunpowder temper can explode in his face when he least expects it. If he makes her angry enough, she will hit him with her fists like a man. He suspects she might even attack him with a sword.

People whisper that Granuaile is a better man than Richard Bourke. This should make him angry, but he is secretly proud. Who else has such a wife?

On one of his visits to Rockfleet, Richard sees her practising with an Italian wheel-lock pistol she has acquired on one of her voyages. Granuaile has set up a row of targets beyond the kitchens – bundles of straw tied together in a manlike shape. Taking the heavy pistol in both hands, she braces herself. She squints her eyes, bites her lip, holds her breath and fires. Her aim is deadly.

She looks up and sees Richard watching. 'Can you shoot as well as this?' she asks.

'I could if I wanted.'

'Show me.' She hands him the pistol. He struggles with the mechanism. At first it will not fire, then suddenly it bucks violently in his hand. The shot goes wild.

'No wonder the English defeated you in Iar Connacht,' Granuaile drawls.

At that moment Richard hates her. But not enough to turn his back and walk away.

At Christmas, 1573, Tibbott, now six years old, is summoned to Rockfleet.

Granuaile and Richard always invite the Bourkes of Carra to celebrate the feast of Christ's birth at Rockfleet.

The guests will gobble down a small herd of cattle and an astonishing number of honey cakes. Granuaile provides many casks of wine and brandy for them as well. 'If we are lucky,' she remarks to Richard, 'they will not burn down the banqueting hall again this year.'

Before the feast begins, she slips away to take a boat across the bay to her father's stronghold at Belclare. Toby is being raised by Anglo-Normans, but she wants him to remember what it means to be Irish.

The boy sits quietly in the boat, watching his mother with large eyes. She is almost like a creature of legend to him. Being with her is very exciting and a little frightening.

At Belclare, preparations for the feast of Christmas begin with special prayers on the first day of Advent. They are conducted in the family chapel by the Abbot of Murrisk, who inherited the office from his father. Meanwhile there has been a mighty cleaning and sweeping of the castle. A stone fort, Belclare was built for protection rather than show, but in this season it is beautiful. Garlands and swags of greenery decorate the walls. Above the main doorway is a timber cross covered with holly sprigs. The collecting of ivy and holly is the special duty of the children of the household. Granuaile urges Toby to take part. At first he is shy, but soon he is whooping and laughing with his cousins.

At sunset on Christmas Eve the family visits nearby Murrisk Abbey. Hundreds of candles are lit to hold the night at bay while they await the anniversary of the Christ child's birth. Next morning they attend a private Mass in the family chapel, and then return to the abbey for a second Mass with as many of their clan as can crowd inside.

Afterwards Granuaile introduces Toby to everyone. 'Tibbott of the Long Ships,' she says. '*My* son.'

They fast until dinner, when the women 'bring in the Christmas'. Cod and ling and sea trout and pickled herring, oysters and scallops and crab and lobster. Eels boiled in milk and dullisk baked into a pudding, with honey and dried berries. Barnacle goose and roast venison are great favourites. The finest wines and brandies are poured out for the aging Black Oak and his kinsmen.

'I imported those,' Granuaile reminds them with a smile. She feels that she must stamp her mark on everything: her son, her imports, her castles. Mine.

After the feast Granuaile's half-brother, Donal, sounds the pipes to announce that the entertainments are about to begin. At an Irish Christmas, solemn prayer and joyous song go hand in hand. Both are pleasing in the sight of God. Toby falls asleep very late indeed.

A week later, as they return across the bay to Rockfleet, Granuaile signals to the boatmen to rest their oars. She stands in the currach, looking back toward Belclare. A wind is rising; the New Year will start with a storm. She does not notice the weather. Her heart is still with her family, with her father.

In her memory Dubhdara has always been huge and strong, but this Christmas he is smaller than she is. His face is caving in upon itself. Her mother is shrinking too; shrinking away.

'Shrinking,' Granuaile murmurs to herself. She dislikes the word. It reminds her that the English are taking great bites out of Ireland. Shrinking the Gaelic world.

A shudder runs through the tall woman, despite her heavy woollen cloak. Her son notices and reaches out a hand to her. She takes it, flicks him a smile, and sits down beside him. At her signal the boatmen resume rowing. The currach skims across the water toward Rockfleet.

But her eyes keep turning back to Belclare.

besieged

In 1574 Rockfleet proves its worth.

Five years earlier the English she-king had appointed a man called Sir Edward Fitton to be governor of Connacht. The title gives him great authority in the territory.

The merchants of Galway have been complaining to Fitton about Granuaile. They claim that by attacking ships destined for their port she is destroying their livelihood. In March of 1574, Fitton sends several ships loaded with men-at-arms to Clew Bay. Granuaile's own vessels have not yet put to sea. The English sail boldly into the inlet at the foot of Rockfleet. By laying siege to the pirate queen's stronghold, they intend to force her to surrender. Then they can kill her and put an end to her raiding.

Thanks to the view from the ramparts, Granuaile is aware of them long before they arrive. This gives her time to prepare her defences.

She always has men garrisoned at Rockfleet. At her order they bring enough barrels of fresh water into the tower to supply the occupants for many weeks. There are adequate stores of food already. Granuaile posts armed men on the ramparts and at every loophole. Then she arms herself with her favourite Italian pistol and waits for the invaders.

The inlet below Rockfleet is shallow. An Irish currach or galley can come right up to the foot of the castle, but English ships have a deeper draft. They have to stand off and fire from a distance. They soon learn how futile this is. Blunderbuss and matchlock are useless against the stone tower. If they had brought warships capable of carrying cannon they might have done damage, but such large ships cannot make their way among the many islands of Clew Bay.

While the English are besieging Rockfleet, Granuaile's men on Clare Island take to their galleys and come in behind them. The English find themselves trapped. After a frantic skirmish, they weigh anchor. Instead of killing Granuaile, they barely escape with their own lives.

She stands on the ramparts of Rockfleet, shading her eyes with her hand. In the far distance she can just make out the English ships. They are still running like hares before the hounds.

A faint smile touches her lips. Expands. Becomes a grin. Becomes a laugh, a great, belly-shaking guffaw that rings out across Clew Bay. Still laughing, Granuaile raises her arm and shakes her fist at the English as they disappear over the horizon.

'Go back where you came from!' she shouts after them. 'This land is ours!'

chapter eight

RELIGIOUS PERSECUTION

Elizabeth Tudor's father, King Henry VIII, had been a Catholic. He had wanted to divorce his wife but the Catholic Church did not permit divorce. The king had tried to persuade the pope to make an exception for him. When the pope refused, Henry had turned his back on his Church.

Meanwhile Protestantism was gaining favour in Europe. It denied the authority of the pope and accepted the Bible as the only word of God. This concept exactly suited Henry Tudor's purpose. He founded his own Protestant church, which allowed him to divorce.

King Henry's daughter Elizabeth was raised in the new faith. Now that she is queen, she has proclaimed herself head of the Church of England. The Protestant religion is to be 'the established faith'. The crosses and candles of Catholicism are being stripped from the altars. Churches are being closed all over Britain and Ireland. The worship of the Virgin Mary is to be replaced by the authority of the Virgin Queen.

April, the Year of Our Lord 1574, Belclare

My dear Toby,

I am so distressed I can hardly put quill to parchment. The English have suppressed the abbey at Murrisk. That abbey was built by my clan over a hundred years ago for the Augustinian friars. Saint Patrick's own Black Bell was housed within its walls. No foreign monarch has any right to close the abbey and strip it of its treasures!

Yet Elizabeth Tudor has signed an order and our abbey is lost.

Is this revenge against me? Is this the way the English queen reacts to a good battle cleanly won?

My first instinct was to attack, to sail to Galway and fall on her officials with sword and pistol. My father said a violent response would only cause more trouble for our clan. The abbot agreed. 'This is the working of God's will,' he assured me. 'All will come right in time.'

Will it? I wonder. But we must have faith.

Always,

Granuaile

Granuaile does not care what religion foreign monarchs follow. That is their business. But to deny Ireland its Catholic faith is monstrous. Even the Anglo-Normans are unhappy. There are rumours of rebellion.

With the closure of Murrisk Abbey, a stone settles in the heart of Granuaile.

donal o'flaherty

In May of 1574, Granuaile returns to sea.

Her father makes her promise to avoid Galway, and she agrees. 'But I cannot avoid all of Iar Connacht,' she tells him. 'You understand that I have responsibilities there.'

The old man bows his head. 'If there is anything in my life I repent, it is the fact that I urged you to marry Donal O'Flaherty.'

'That was as much my mother's fault as yours. When I was sixteen, an age when most women are already wed, I was still as wild as a leaping dolphin. Mother despaired of me. She kept urging you to arrange a suitable match for me and at last you suggested *Donal-an-Chogaidh*, Donal of the Battles. You thought he would make a fine husband because he was tanaiste of Clan O'Flaherty, from Iar Connacht to the south.'

'I knew nothing of him personally,' Dubhdara hastens to say. 'The clan had a fearsome reputation but we had never had trouble with them.'

'That may have been because a range of mountains separated us from them,' Granuaile replies. 'When Donal first came to Clare Island I was not very impressed. He was a sour little man who strutted like a cockerel and had bad teeth. But he assured you that he would provide well for me, and he swore that our clans would be allies forever. The last part is true at least. That is why I must go back to Iar Connacht from time to time.'

Granuaile often thought of Iar Connacht and the years when she had lived there as a member of Clan O'Flaherty. They were not happy memories, but they had made her the woman she was. Fire tempers steel.

After their marriage Donal had taken Granuaile to live in Bunowen Castle, beside a narrow tidal inlet that provides access to a fine bay and the sea beyond. On the day she arrived she noticed a number of boats pulled up on the shore. They looked badly neglected. She walked down to the water's edge and stared at them. They were rotting like the seaweed on the strand.

It seemed a terrible waste, but Donal had refused to explain. He bristled like a pig and acted as if his new wife had no right to question him. Being Granuaile, she did not accept this. She went privately to talk with the cottagers who lived around Bunowen, and learned the truth soon enough.

For centuries the O'Flaherties had used the sea as much as the O'Malleys did. Sailing out of Galway, Connacht's most important seaport, Donal's people had travelled up and down the west coast of Ireland. They did some fishing, but their main source of income was the plunder they took by raiding. They kept the best and traded the rest in Galway's markets.

The New English had arrived in southwestern Iar Connacht a generation earlier. Helped by the Anglo-Norman merchants in Galway, they had set themselves up in the city and barred the gates against the native Irish. The ferocious O'Flaherties were no longer welcome in Galway town.

At first Clan O'Flaherty had fought back, but the foreigners guarded the port with warships and cannon. After a time the O'Flaherties gave up. A strong leader could have put heart in them, but the chief of the clan, known as The O'Flaherty, was not a young man. His chosen successor, Granuaile's new husband, was not a strong leader. Donal preferred to sulk. He blamed everyone but himself for his troubles. He never kept allies for long and had no friends.

Donal's holdings included two fortresses, one at Bunowen and the other at Ballinahinch. Granuaile was expected to supervise the servants and supplies for both castles. When she investigated their stores, she was shocked to discover how poor her new family was. No gold, no silk, no glassware. Linen sheets for the beds but they were ragged. On Clew Bay, Granuaile's people wanted for nothing. Donal's people buttered their bread with want.

Since they no longer took to the sea, they were forced to live off the corn they raised, and their sheep and cattle. Iar Connacht was a rugged land and corn and cattle did not always thrive. Sheep fared better. Irish wool was prized abroad. Unfortunately the English had banned the export of fleeces from Galway.

So, in spite of the glowing claims Donal had made to Dubhdara, the O'Flaherties were no longer prosperous. That did not stop Donal from acting like the high king of Ireland. He swanned around, boasting of past glories and provoking quarrels with his neighbours, while Granuaile pared the cheese ever thinner and added more water to the wine. The soles of her leather shoes wore so thin she threw them away and began walking barefoot again, as she had in childhood.

At first she tried to be a good wife by modelling herself on her mother. Dubhdara was a kind man who provided well and did not mistreat his wife. But Granuaile's experience with Donal was very different. He was often insulting and always mean. He did not physically abuse her, though. Not after the first time he had tried. When he had doubled up his fist to hit her, she had hit him first and knocked him down.

Granuaile bore Donal O'Flaherty three children: Owen, Murrough, and Margaret. Even three babies were not enough to exhaust her energy. She cast longing eyes toward the sea, remembering the days when she was free and life seemed boundless.

After Margaret was born, Granuaile grew sick of

eating boiled mutton. Although she could not see them, she sensed vast schools of fish in the bay. Even when she was indoors she could tell whether the tide was rising, whether the herring were running, and which way the wind blew.

As part of her dowry she had brought a fine currach. She appointed four of Donal's men to row and took her boat out. They glimpsed English warships on the far horizon but Granuaile refused to be frightened. She stood upright in the prow and held her arms wide. 'How splendid it is to be on the water again, gliding along like a seahorse!' she exclaimed.

When they returned at sundown, the boat was laden to the gunwales with silvery fish. The people on the shore observed the catch with envy. Granuaile divided most of the fish among them. Shyly, they asked if she would help revive their neglected fleet.

'I did more than help,' she wrote to her father some months later. 'Within a short time I have taken charge. I can see what needs to be done; I know how to make decisions. From you I learned to give men encouragement rather than harsh words.'

Before Donal knew what was happening, his followers were deserting him for Granuaile. Under her command, they began building new galleys and sailing around the coast. Granuaile traded O'Flaherty fish for luxury goods. These were in great demand but in short supply around the west of Ireland. The English were demanding high tolls for any cargo brought into Galway.

By avoiding Galway altogether, Granuaile could sell imported merchandise elsewhere for lower prices.

Great lords and clan chieftains bought everything she had to sell. In southern waters she obtained an ostrich egg fitted with a silver spout so that it could be used as a drinking beaker. Granuaile had never heard of an ostrich. Neither had the Anglo-Norman nobleman who bought it from her, but he gave her a purse full of gold for the pretty bauble.

For the first time in years, the O'Flahertys greased their knives with fat. Women blessed Granuaile's name and children ran to hug her knees.

Instead of being grateful, her husband was jealous of her achievement. When she tried to explain that he had thrown away his opportunities, he would not listen. He accused Granuaile of treachery.

Yet she never abandoned Donal's people. She never would.

chapter ten

homecoming

When she married Donal O'Flaherty, Granuaile had thought she would spend her life in Iar Connacht.

Moor and mountain. Stony earth heaved up like ocean waves. Standing water everywhere, and a constant change of light and colour when the clouds broke to make way for the sun. Then the hillsides were transformed to dazzling green, or mottled in mauve and dark gold. A moment later and the sun would vanish, leaving the scene awash in shades of purple. This land at the edge of the Atlantic shared many of the great ocean's moods and mysteries. Granuaile could have loved Iar Connacht if only she could have loved Donal-an-Chogaidh.

He had made that impossible. Donal could not accept the fact that his wife, a mere female, was responsible for his new prosperity. He constantly belittled Granuaile in front of others. Yet, although he resented her success, he was more than willing to accept the treasure she brought home.

The chieftain of Iar Connacht had been elected by his people in accordance with Gaelic law. He was known as The O'Flaherty and had named Donal-an-Chogaidh as his tanaiste. But if The O'Flaherty died, Donal would have to be confirmed by another election before he could claim the title.

Unfortunately Donal was not a popular man, and he knew it. He adopted two policies to gain support: bribery and battle. He had observed how well bribery worked for the English. Those Donal could not bribe, he attacked. He needed more warriors, he needed gold to buy more weapons, he needed, he needed. His demands were endless.

Granuaile did her best to meet them. She built strong new galleys and began attacking merchant ships on their way to Galway. Since the English had closed the port to the O'Flaherties, she felt it was only fair. The men were overjoyed. They raised a loud cheer in Granuaile's name each morning before they set sail, and at night they remembered her in their prayers. Her name was given to their daughters.

When Donal accused her of stealing the love of his people she told him, 'All I have done is remind them of who they are. I have given them their pride back. Without that, one has nothing.'

'You have enough pride for ten,' Donal snapped. 'Someday I hope it will destroy you.'

As her children grew older, her husband's temper grew worse. Granuaile spent most of her time on shipboard. While she was at sea a member of the O'Flaherty clan, Murrough of the Battle-Axes, began troubling the land. He was young, strong and even fonder of battle than Donal-an-Chogaidh. Murrough led his followers as far south as Thomond and the barony of Clare. There he won a great victory over the Anglo-Norman earl of Clanrickard. Many men were slain.

Clanrickard complained to the English, reminding them of his relationship with the Crown. He demanded support against Murrough of the Battle-Axes. But rather than face Murrough on the battlefield, the English set out to buy him. In return for his submission they named him chieftain of Iar Connacht – The O'Flaherty. The old chieftain was stripped of his title without his people having anything to say about it.

Donal was wild with fury. Granuaile tried to calm him before he did something foolish. 'If the English can overthrow Gaelic law and unmake our elected chieftains,' she said, 'they now have more power than we do. Be cautious, husband. Bide your time and plan carefully before you act.'

But Donal O'Flaherty was incapable of planning carefully.

One of the leading Anglo-Norman families in Connacht was the Joyce clan. They were profiting mightily from the port of Galway, so they made a great noise about supporting the English – and Murrough of the Battle-Axes.

For all his bold talk, Donal-an-Chogaidh was not

quite brave enough to attack the English. Instead he declared that he would kill every Joyce within a day's march.

Donal launched a surprise attack upon a Joyce stronghold at Lough Corrib. Anger strengthens the arm. He succeeded in driving out the Joyces and occupying their castle, which stood on an island in the lake. Donal set a guard around the castle and then sent for Granuaile. He wanted to show her what he had accomplished without her help.

She found her husband strutting around the place, dressed in his finest clothes. 'I am the cock of the castle now!' he boasted.

'You have only a toehold here,' she warned him. 'I know something of strategy, and I suggest you secure the lakeshore nearest the island.'

But Donal's head was swollen with victory. 'Why should I listen to a woman's blatherings? The Joyces will not dare to come back. They know I have bested them.'

A few days later he left the island to go hunting in the woods on the shore. There the Joyces caught and killed him. The cheer they raised rang across the lake.

With Donal O'Flaherty dead, the Joyces thought his men would panic and surrender the castle to them. From the ramparts, Granuaile could see them putting boats in the water and rowing toward the island.

She met them with a battle-axe and a loaded musket.

Donal's men fell in behind her, and together they slew many of the Joyces. The few survivors barely made it back to their boats. 'Tell your kinsmen that Granuaile holds this island now!' Donal's widow called to their fleeing backs.

Since that day, the castle in Lough Corrib has been known as The Hen's Castle.

Granuaile mourned her husband to the exact degree required by tradition, but no more. She hired the best keening women to grieve publicly. But she did not tear her hair, nor did she rend her clothes. 'Men often die in battle,' she was heard to remark.

By killing the Joyces she had made dangerous enemies. Sooner or later they would come after her. Granuaile was not willing to sit with folded hands and wait for them.

By this time her sons were grown and going their own way. One was living at Bunowen, the other at Ballinahinch. When the old, former O'Flaherty chieftain took up arms to challenge Murrough of the Battles, they joined him.

Meanwhile, Granuaile's daughter Margaret had become betrothed to one of the Bourkes, a man known as The Devil's Hook. The nickname came from his territory of Curraun on Achill Island. With Margaret married, there was nothing to keep Granuaile in Iar Connacht any longer.

'I am free to return to Umhall Uí Mháille,' she wrote to her father, Dubhdara. 'I am coming home.'

Two hundred of Donal's men chose to go with her.

For Granuaile, it was an unforgettable homecoming. The years since have not dimmed its bright memory.

When the fleet from the south first appeared on the horizon, a lookout on Clare Island raised a shout of alarm. 'The O'Flaherties are coming!' Even if they were allies, one could never be certain. This might be a raid.

Then observers noticed a banner fluttering in the prow of the lead galley. It was not the flag of the O'Flaherties, with its red lions. This one showed a white seahorse against a blue ground.

'Granuaile!' a man shouted suddenly. He threw off his cloak and began waving it over his head in welcome.

Granuaile did not make landfall at Clare Island. She swept into Clew Bay and made straight for the anchorage at Belclare.

Her father, the man they called the Black Oak, was no longer young, no longer strong. Yet he stood as straight as ever on the shore. His wife was beside him. Soon Granuaile's half-brother, Donal of the Pipes, arrived hot-foot from his fort at Cathair-na-Mart to share in the celebration of her return.

She did not wait for her boat to be beached, but leaped out and waded through the shallows, holding up her skirts, splashing and laughing. Granuaile had left Clew Bay as a girl. She returned as a woman. A lean, muscular, windburnt woman, her heavy black hair parted in the middle and wearing gold Spanish bracelets from wrist to elbow.

Dubhdara noticed that the men who accompanied her stayed respectfully behind her. The cast of their faces marked them as O'Flaherties.

She greeted her father and mother lovingly, then nodded a greeting to her half-brother, who was gaping at her with his mouth ajar. Her dark eyes twinkled with amusement at his surprise. Then she turned back to her father.

'I have come back to stay, Dubhdara,' she said.

That night in the great hall at Belclare she heard the latest news. The O'Malleys were still fiercely independent. But the English were demanding that The MacWilliam pay rent on land the Bourke clan had held for generations. Dubhdara was furious. 'This is extortion! Why should anyone pay money to foreigners in order to live on their own land?'

Granuaile took a long, thoughtful drink from the pewter tankard she held. 'Elizabeth Tudor has a long reach,' she said.

A few days later the O'Malleys gave a huge banquet to celebrate Granuaile's homecoming. People came from all around Clew Bay. One of the guests was Richard Bourke, the man known as Richard-in-Iron.

chapter eleven
a pirate at work

Usually spring on the Atlantic is a season of winds and storms. The year of 1575 is different. The sun is uncommonly frequent, and the sea is uncommonly quiet. Summer arrives before its time, with gathering heat and heavy, still air.

The first of the summer merchantmen is becalmed just outside Clew Bay.

Standing in the prow of her favourite galley, Granuaile lifts her arm and points toward the vessel. 'See there!' she shouts to her men. 'With her hold so full of cargo she rides low in the water, our prey is waiting!'

The broad-beamed Dutch cargo ship is laying on all the sail it has, but the canvas hangs limp in the moist still air. The rowers grunt like pigs as they beat the water with their oars. They cannot hope to outrun the Irish galleys.

Granuaile's fleet encircles them as hounds encircle a wild boar.

The skirmish is brisk and brief. Within half an hour, the she-king of the western seas stands on the deck of the

Dutch ship. Her men are shifting the cargo to their own boats. They are laughing and jesting. The Dutch sailors, who have nothing to laugh about, stand sullenly watching. If they are lucky they will escape with their lives.

The captain of the ship is a stocky Dutchman with a broad, red face. He still cannot quite believe he has been boarded by a woman. It is humiliating. He shakes his fist at her and she laughs.

No woman has ever laughed at him before, and certainly not on his own ship. A muscle jumps in his jaw.

When the last packing case has been transferred to the waiting galleys, Granuaile leaps nimbly down onto her flagship. 'Thank you for your generosity!' she calls to the Dutchman. He does not understand Irish but he understands insult. As the galley pulls away he runs to his cabin and returns with a pistol. He props both his arms on the gunwale and takes careful aim. The distance between the two ships is swiftly widening, but he is a good shot.

And lucky.

❦ ❦ ❦

June, the Year of Our Lord 1575, Clare Island

My dear Toby,

At this season I am usually at sea. A slight injury – nothing you need worry about – is keeping me on the island a little longer. My shoulder is giving me some trouble but my right hand is undamaged, thank God. So I can write to you.

Are you well, my son? Are the priests teaching you as I have instructed them? Learn your letters, study Latin, and memorise the names of the major seaports. Your older brothers by Donal O'Flaherty are merely simple warriors, all strength and shouting. I want more than that for you. Against an enemy as powerful as the English it is necessary to fight with one's brain. Fortunately you and I both inherited good brains.

It saddens me to tell you that my beloved Dubhdara is dying. Your grandfather is like an ancient oak tree that has fallen in the forest and is slowly crumbling away. I continue to captain the fleet and support his people. I cannot say what the future holds, but be assured I shall do my best.

Always,

Granuaile

CHAPTER TWELVE

THE LONG ARM OF ELIZABETH

A year later, Sir Henry Sidney arrives in Connacht with a large force of soldiers. He demands that the Irish chieftains and Anglo-Norman lords come to meet him in Galway at once. If they refuse, their land and property will be seized.

Richard Bourke, as leader of one branch of the Bourke clan, is not considered important enough to be summoned to Galway. The MacWilliam, chief of all the Bourkes, goes, however. In addition to his earlier submission, this time he agrees to uphold English law in Mayo and to raise an army of two hundred men in the name of the Crown. In return for his promises The MacWilliam is granted a knighthood.

Richard Bourke is jealous, but Granuaile is contemptuous. 'Earldoms. Knighthoods. Apparently with a wave of her hand Elizabeth can make anyone noble, even a fool or a scoundrel!' she says.

Dubhdara's kinsman Melaghlin has been elected chieftain of the O'Malleys. He travels to Galway and gives the submission Dubhdara never would. Melaghlin claims it is the only way he can protect O'Malley lands from seizure. He says he has no choice.

But Granuaile refuses to believe that. There is always a choice.

The English she-king may have forced an O'Malley submission. But she did not get one from Granuaile.

Most of the Irish are indifferent to the growing power of Elizabeth Tudor. At one time, Ireland had more than two hundred tribal kings. These owed loyalty to their provincial kings, who in turn acknowledged a high king as overlord. It made little difference to the common people. Their lives were the same no matter who ruled.

They do not expect things to change under a monarch who lives far away.

Granuaile does not accept the situation so calmly. She has observed the English taking control of Iar Connacht by overthrowing Gaelic law. The new order has not been created for the benefit of Irish people.

The English are gnawing away at their freedom, bit by bit.

When Richard Bourke comes to visit her at Rockfleet, Granuaile lies awake at night listening to him snore. She is amazed that he can sleep so deeply. She does not sleep well any more, but his snoring is not the problem.

Staring up into the gloom above the bed, Granuaile tries to imagine the face of Elizabeth of England.

chapter thirteen

kidnap

September, the Year of Our Lord 1576, Rockfleet

My dear Toby,

I have played the most marvellous prank on one of Elizabeth's lords. You will enjoy this.

The purpose of my most recent voyage to Scotland was to bring back Scottish gallowglasses for Hugh Dubh O'Donnell, chief of Tyrconnell. Gallowglasses are huge and fearsome mercenaries. O'Donnell's wife, a daughter of the earl of Argyll, insists they are the best fighting men in the world. She may be right. I have made a small fortune importing them for the northern chieftains.

Returning from Scotland, I called in at Dublin port to resupply my fleet before sailing for Ulster and home. While I waited for my ships to be loaded, I went to call upon the lord of Howth and request hospitality. I expected Christopher St Lawrence to uphold the Irish tradition, as most of the Anglo-Normans do.

When I arrived I found the gates of Howth Castle

62

locked. The gatekeeper told me that Lord St Lawrence was at his dinner and would not be disturbed. Imagine!

As I was going back down the road toward the harbour I chanced upon a boy playing. A dear little lad, with bright eyes and rosy cheeks. He reminded me of you. I stopped to chat with him and discovered that he was the lord's son. So I took him away with me.

When we returned to Clew Bay I sent a message to the high and mighty Lord St Lawrence. I told him I was holding his son hostage. He hurried to Mayo, which he had never seen before and is unlikely to visit again. The lord of Howth came to Rockfleet in a most humble way, it did my heart good to see his improved attitude.

The boy would be returned safely, I said, upon receipt of St Lawrence's promise that the gates of his castle would never again be closed against anyone requesting hospitality. Furthermore, an extra place must always to be set at table in case I should return. The lord of Howth agreed to my demands most eagerly.

He gave me a heavy gold ring in pledge of our pact. Irish red gold, I noticed. Taken from ourselves no doubt.

I entertained St Lawrence as he should have entertained me, with platters heaped high and goblets overflowing. Then I sent him home with his son – whom he loves as much as I love mine.

Always,
Granuaile

◉ ◉ ◉

The sense of defiance is growing in Granuaile. She has brought one of the great lords to heel, made him come crawling to her. It is a heady feeling.

She continues to use the sea for fishing and trading, but also begins raiding farmsteads along the coast. Granuaile never attacks O'Malleys or Bourkes, but anyone else who is friendly with the New English can expect an unpleasant visit.

She works her way around the hinterlands of Clew Bay, capturing a castle here, a stronghold there. She takes control of the island of Inishbofin, where merchant ships stop to take on fresh water. Granuaile begins charging them for the water. She also impounds the boats of the islanders. Deprived of their means of livelihood, the men of Inishbofin elect to join Granuaile.

Her raiding intensifies.

New complaints against the pirate queen pour in to the governor of Connacht, Sir Henry Sidney.

negotiating with the enemy

In February of 1577 Henry Sidney marches on Castle Barry, the stronghold of Edmund Bourke. Edmund Bourke has long resisted the New English. Sidney seizes his castle and gives it to Shane MacOliverus, The MacWilliam. The message is obvious – the Bourkes who surrender will be rewarded, the rest will suffer.

Sidney's deed splits the Bourke clan. Granuaile admits to herself that it is good military strategy.

'No English man with grasping hands will ever enter the portal of Rockfleet,' Granuaile says defiantly to Richard-in-Iron, 'because this castle is no longer a Bourke holding. Not since you surrendered it to me.'

'You are a clever woman,' he replies, amused rather than angry.

'Richard, we must go together and meet Sidney when he returns to Galway.'

He is astonished. 'Sidney will not see you. A mere woman!'

Richard has never understood Granuaile. But he no longer argues with her.

Taking three of her largest galleys and two hundred fighting men, a mixed force of O'Malleys and O'Flaherties, they sail boldly into Galway Bay. The English understand bribes. They will surely recognise the value of this one.

Granuaile and Richard are shown into the castle where Sir Henry Sidney has his apartments. It is a cold, dark, gloomy place with a vile odour. Granuaile cannot help wrinkling her nose in distaste. She is used to having the sea wind in her nostrils. The New English do not bathe and every place they occupy smells sour.

Sidney has seen any number of major and minor chieftains, but he has never before faced an Irish woman who leads men in her own right. Granuaile strides into his audience chamber with her head high, as befits a she-king. As far as Granuaile is concerned, Sidney is an underling.

He sits behind a long oaken table piled high with documents. His clothing is dusty and his eyes are tired. 'He is not as big as I expected,' Granuaile whispers to Richard behind her hand.

Speaking to Sidney in the Latin tongue they both understand, she tells him that she knows the exact number of Elizabeth's ships and the size and armaments of their crews. 'They are not enough to subdue this coast,' she assures him. 'Not if the seafaring tribes of the west stand against you.'

It is a bluff, but Granuaile is a trader who long ago learned the art of bluffing. Fortunately Sidney cannot hear her heart pounding beneath her cloak. 'I command both the O'Malley and the O'Flaherty fleets,' she adds. 'I am sure you know of our many successes in sea battles.'

Sidney is watching her very carefully. He does not once look past her to Richard, who stands in silence behind her.

At last the Englishman props his elbows on the table and leans forward. 'I have heard of you, Grace O'Malley,' he pronounces her name in the English way. 'You are a notorious woman in all the coasts of Ireland.'

Granuaile does not disagree.

'I have come to offer you three galleys and two hundred men,' she says calmly. 'They will be a great asset. I am sure you would rather have them with you than against you.'

He nods, slowly. 'What do you ask in return?'

'Simply to be left alone in my own place. There is nothing of value for you in Clew Bay. A few stone forts, fishing grounds, a goodly amount of seaweed – I am certain you have more to gain elsewhere, and for less effort.'

Sidney nods again. 'All you ask is to be left alone?'

'That is all.'

He rubs his chin. 'I suppose it is not too much to ask.'

Clew Bay is nothing to him, Granuaile tells herself. *But it is the world to me.*

chapter fifteen
a bold plan

The morning is radiant. Granuaile leaves the tower house on Clare Island to walk along the headland, gazing out over the water. Clew Bay has never looked more beautiful to her. She has pitted her wits against the foreigners and succeeded. There are no English warships at the mouth of the bay. The O'Malleys can fish and trade without hindrance. The Bourke holdings around the shore are undisturbed.

Tibbott, miles away in Kinturk Castle, can sleep safely in his bed.

She descends the narrow path to the tiny inlet below the tower house. This is her private bay, one of her favourite places. A crescent of pure white sand slopes into water the colour of a peacock's tail. It is so clear she can see the individual grains of sand on the bottom. Granuaile always has a small boat or two hidden away in the caves that ring the inlet.

She stands for a long time, musing. The sun is warm on her head. The sea birds cry, adding their voices to that of the wind. Otherwise all is silent. It might be a thousand years ago or a thousand years from now. And she is a part of it.

It is time to take out the fishing fleet. As she makes her preparations, Granuaile can feel the tide rising in the bay. Even with her eyes closed, she knows the exact conditions of the sea.

But they will change tomorrow.

Her eyes open abruptly.

The water is very calm. A few gentle swells, nothing more. Yet there is a faint, unpleasant scent on the wind. A sour smell. Suddenly Granuaile throws up her head, every sense quivering.

✦   ✦   ✦

April, the Year of Our Lord 1577, Clare Island

Dear Toby,

Sidney has promised that my people and I will be left alone, but I do not believe him. When a little time has passed he will think of some reason to invade Umhall Ui Mhaille. I know it as I know when the herring are running.

I must convince the English that I am too strong to challenge. Murrough of the Battle-Axes did this and gained a chieftaincy. I have no desire for an illegal title awarded by foreigners. I only want to impress the English with my power.

A bold plan has occurred to me. Instead of fishing, I am going to sail south along the coast as far as Limerick.

69

The earl of Desmond counts all that territory as his. He is one of the great Anglo-Norman overlords like Clanrickard or the earl of Ormond. Many years ago, when one of the English kings was trying to conquer Ireland, he awarded their ancestors vast tracts of Irish land in return for their services. Now they rule those lands like kings themselves. During my years of trade I have sold many luxury goods to them, so I know.

A successful raid against one of the great lords should convince the English that I am a force to be respected.

We will sail up the Shannon until we find a safe anchorage. There are many little inlets along the great river. Surely one of them will be so isolated that no one will see us. Guards will be posted to stay with the boats while I take the rest of my men inland. Raiding ashore is unlike sea raiding, Toby. On land we must advance under cover of darkness or hide ourselves in the forest. Otherwise our prey will be warned. It is important to keep the element of surprise. This rule has served me well on the sea and should be just as true on land.

The sea is familiar territory. I can never master the sea but I understand her. The land is a new challenge, a challenge I shall enjoy.

Always,
Granuaile

chapter sixteen

attacking the great earl

The sky is black velvet. Granuaile has waited deliberately for dark of the moon. She signals to her men to advance cautiously. Twigs crackle underfoot. Leafless branches claw at them like fingers. She passes the word to be as quiet as possible. The clink of metal weapons could give them away. However, they seem to be alone in the night.

Their first venture into Desmond territory is already a success. Granuaile and her men have raided the outlying holdings of the earl's kinsmen and seized quantities of plunder. Porters have carried great loads of furs, grain, and leathers back to the waiting galleys in the Shannon, to transport to Clew Bay.

Granuaile has not gone back to Mayo with the ships. They were ordered to unload their cargo and return immediately. She plans to have an even larger treasure waiting for them when they arrive.

Together with a handpicked force of her best fighting men, on this night she is striking into Desmond's very heart.

The earl's principle residence is Askeaton Castle, which occupies a rocky limestone island in the Deel River. The castle is a typical Norman design. The island is encircled with a stone wall and guarded by a watch-tower at the southern end. Another stone wall, or bailey, encloses a central court, and a great keep stands on the northern end. The fortress looks too strong to capture, but Granuaile knows better. Any castle so large must have a weakness somewhere.

Desmond himself is away, perhaps in England. Granuaile imagines him grovelling before Elizabeth. Bowing his head. A hound pleading to be petted rather than kicked. She feels contempt for him.

In the earl's absence, Askeaton's guards may be careless. The raiding party is counting on it. Granuaile intends to attack the castle and carry Desmond's treas-ures home to Rockfleet in triumph. If he wants them back, let him come crawling to her as the lord of Howth crawled for his son.

A mighty tide surges through her veins. This is better than wine or mead or even strong French brandy. Granuaile is intoxicated.

The dark outline of the castle looms ahead. She pauses to take a deep breath and enjoy the moment. Then she gives the signal.

chapter seventeen

Limerick gaol

Granuaile and her men approach the outer wall of Desmond's stronghold under cover of darkness. They are delighted to find a postern gate unguarded. As quick as thought they rush through. Before the last of them clears the opening they are surrounded.

Too late, they realise that the open gate was a trap.

Desmond's men are well armed with swords and muskets. Granuaile has always valued the element of surprise, but this time she is the one surprised. Although her band fights valiantly it is no use. They are greatly outnumbered.

Among Desmond's men are native Irishmen whose services have been purchased with the earl's gold. Granuaile even recognises some Scottish gallowglasses fighting beside the Old English. She screams her rage and attacks the nearest man.

Her men are falling, dying all around her. Yet miraculously, or so it seems at the time, no one shoots or stabs Granuaile. Desmond's men are careful to take her alive.

She is thrown into the dungeon of Askeaton Castle. No food is brought to her, nor water, until the next day. Then she is treated like a hound that will not hunt. Her gaolers curse at her and kick her when they can get close enough. They tell her nothing of the fate of her men. They will not answer any questions at all.

Time passes, but she does not know how much. She is too dazed.

When she is weak with hunger Granuaile is bound hand and foot, slung across the back of a horse and taken to Limerick town. For the first time she sees some of her men. At least two have survived. They are tied together and marched along behind her horse. When one of them stumbles, he is beaten.

By the time they reach Limerick Granuaile feels as if her ribs are crushed. But there is worse to come. She and her men are dragged up before an English magistrate who sentences them to prison. For her crimes, Granuaile is condemned to stay in Limerick Gaol for eighteen months. Or more, as the queen sees fit.

● ● ●

June, the Year of Our Lord 1577, Limerick Gaol

My dear Toby,

I pray that this letter reaches you. One of my gaolers was sympathetic when I told him I had a small son. He had a young lad himself, he said. I pleaded with him to help me send word to you. At last he agreed – if I gave him all the jewellery on my person. Unfortunately I do not wear much when I am raiding. A few gold rings, a brooch set with gemstones. Please God it is enough.

If this message reaches you, please tell your father what has happened. He is not to attempt anything foolish. It would be unbearable if my capture brought punishment upon my people.

Ask Richard to send word to Melaghlin O'Malley as well. And pray for me.

Always,
Granuaile

❖   ❖   ❖

At night she sleeps on a bare stone floor, with no straw under her and no blanket over her. The stones are gritty against her cheek. Rats scuttle through the darkness. Sometimes one, braver than the others, runs across her feet.

In the morning she is so stiff she can hardly move. She makes desperate rowing motions with her elbows as she raises her upper body. Every muscle screams with pain. Her skin and hair are crawling with fleas. Although she claws at her flesh until she brings blood, nothing will stop the itch of the fleabites.

She struggles to her feet and begins to pace the cell. There is nothing else to do, day after day. Three steps this way, three steps back. No animal would be penned in so small a space. There is no window, only a tiny grille through which her gaolers can watch her. Twice a day she is given a small meal of coarse black bread and dried fish. The bread contains small chips of stone left from the milling process. The fish is almost too salty to eat and makes her desperately thirsty. A small, slimy bucket holds the only drinking water. When the bucket is empty it is not refilled until the next day.

Prisoners are the same as hostages, Granuaile thinks. Under Gaelic law, hostages are treated as well as one's own family.

English law is different.

The men captured with her are in another cell in another part of the gaol. She is not allowed to see them. She is not allowed to see anyone. Being alone and isolated is part of her punishment.

Granuaile wants to beat on the door with her fists and howl like a wolf, but she will not give the enemy that satisfaction. From time to time, men come and peer into her cell. Although she can hear the rumble of their voices they do not speak to her. Once she hears someone referred to as 'Lord Fitzgerald' and knows the earl of Desmond himself stands outside. Gloating over his captive.

She clenches her fists but will not call out to him for mercy.

● ● ●

In November, one of her gaolers – the one who had agreed to send her letters to Toby – brings worrying news.

Desmond's loyalty to Elizabeth has long been in question. Great lords act like kings in their own right. The earl's family, the Fitzgeralds, have rebelled against the Crown before. Years ago they even appealed to England's enemies on the continent for help. Desmond himself has been trying to appease the queen of late. To prove that he is a faithful servant of the Crown, he is going to surrender Granuaile to Lord Justice Drury. Drury is the president of Munster and stands very high in Elizabeth's favour.

Granuaile has no idea what Drury will do with her. She is very closely guarded, so there is no possibility of escape. Except in her dreams at night.

In her dreams she goes down to the shore and smells the sea wind. In her dreams she runs barefoot along the strand.

chapter eighteen

the weight of fear

Although Granuaile is now officially in Drury's custody, he leaves her to rot in Limerick Gaol.

Her thoughts are a thunder inside her head.

The weary months drag on. Nothing changes but herself. Until Granuaile was thrown in prison, her active life had kept her as strong as a girl. Now that she is confined in a cramped cell, age is catching up with her. When she holds up one of her arms she sees the flesh sagging from the bone. She feels a hot flash of fury. What remains of youth is being stolen from her!

Smuggled letters from Toby give her hope. 'We are going to try to get you out,' he writes. 'Do not worry, we will be very careful.'

She takes heart, stands taller, imagines herself free.

Nothing happens. Gradually fear becomes a sick lump in her belly. Granuaile wakes with it in the morning, lies down with it at night. But a she-king cannot admit to anyone that she is afraid. It is something she can only whisper to God in the quiet of the night.

Meanwhile Drury writes to Elizabeth's privy council. In the lord justice's letter he describes his captive as 'Granny O'Mayle, a woman that hath impudently passed the part of womanhood and been a great spoiler, and chief commander and director of thieves and murderers at sea.'

The Privy Council commends Desmond for his capture of such a dangerous person. The earl is back in favour. But not for long – he refuses to pay massive taxes and he refuses to accept the Protestant religion. An open war is declared between himself and the Crown, a war that explodes across the face of southern Ireland.

In the far distance, cannon boom. Deep within the walls of her prison, Granuaile cannot hear them.

Winter becomes spring, becomes summer, becomes autumn.

chapter nineteen
dublin castle

November, the Year of Our Lord 1578, Dublin Castle

My dear Toby,

I have exchanged one gaol for another. Drury has sent me to Dublin, where I am given into the custody of the new lord justice. Fortunately I have found someone who agreed to smuggle this letter out to you. I only hope it reaches you.

Together with the two men who were captured with me at Askeaton, I was brought to Dublin in a pony cart. The English feared to transport us by sea, lest my fleet rescue us. We were accompanied by a number of English guards on foot and on horseback. The journey over land was long and tiresome. There is no road across Ireland, merely a network of rutted, often muddy trackways. The cart jounced and jolted me until I felt as if my bones were breaking through my skin. How I missed the broad highway of the sea! But at least I was under open sky again.

I have learned to appreciate such blessings.

As we travelled I saw terrible sights, Toby. Ireland is being destroyed. Desmond's rebellion has resulted in the rich fields of Munster being laid waste. Crops are burned, cattle slaughtered, houses pulled down. Peasants stood a safe distance from the road and shook their fists at us as we passed. They shouted curses upon all foreigners, lords and princes. Our guards ignored them, but I could not. I understood what they were feeling.

When we reached Leinster, we saw garrisons of soldiers everywhere. The farms within the Pale looked prosperous, however, and the houses were not burnt.

People paid little attention to us as we entered the gates of Dublin town. The sight of Irish prisoners arriving in chains has become all too common. Only the urchins in the street noticed me. Once I strode these streets as the respected captain of a fleet. Shop owners paid court to me then, eager for my custom. Now small boys feel free to shout insults. I bit my thumbnail at them, a custom I acquired during my travels.

Dublin Castle is a dreadful place, my son. The sight of it chills the heart. This is no welcoming stronghold in times of trouble. The queen's administrators rule much of Ireland from here with a clenched fist.

The castle is solidly built of stone and surrounded by a deep trench. Over this, a drawbridge gives the only entry to the castle yard. Within the building are countless chambers and airless passageways, barred doorways and locked iron gates. A well-used gallows throws its dark shadow across the filthy cobbles of the inner yard.

The dungeons below the castle ring night and day with cries of despair. People are executed here for crimes much smaller than mine. Many are Palesmen, loyal to the queen. Yet they are called traitors because they cannot pay the high taxes imposed upon them. The queen's government is always desperate for money, it seems. Yet the English have no understanding of the desperation of others.

Just this morning a poor lad no older than you was taken, kicking and screaming, and hanged. He had stolen a wee bit of bread. He cried out that his mother and sisters would die of hunger without him, but the authorities took no notice. They call this English justice! Under Gaelic law he would have been fed if he was starving, and his family too. But our laws are thrown down.

The two men who were brought here with me are being hanged tomorrow. For their loyalty to me they are condemned.

Dublin Castle is a hotbed of rumour. Much of it is nonsense, but one thing is certain. English soldiers are pouring onto this island like a plague of rats. Leinster, Munster, and now even Connaught are under the heel of the foreign queen. Only Ulster continues to resist. If I had my freedom I would go to their aid. I would import guns and mercenaries for Tyrconnell and Tyrone.

I have sent a message to a friend of mine, Black Thomas, the duke of Ormond, for whom I have done a bit of smuggling. I implored him to use whatever influence he has at Elizabeth's court to help me. I have no way of knowing if he ever received my message. One cannot trust anyone in this place.

If God is with me you will hear from me again. In the meantime be brave, my son.

Always,

Granuaile

❋　　❋　　❋

She is awakened before dawn. 'Arthur Wilton de Grey, the new lord deputy of Ireland, has consented to grant you an audience,' a gaoler tells her. 'Prepare yourself.'

Her clothes are rags, and filthy. 'I cannot insult the lord deputy by appearing like this!' Granuaile cries. With an effort, she stands erect and forces her rusty voice to sound strong. Commanding.

Her gaolers exchange glances. They are not accustomed to being given orders by a prisoner. But there is something about this woman …

At last one of them fetches a peasant's gown of coarse homespun that he has taken from some other captive. Granuaile looks at the garment with a mingling of distaste and relief. At least the gown is not badly torn.

She demands that the gaolers leave her cell while she dresses. This they will not do. Turning her back, she strips off her old clothes and pulls the gown over her head. Long months spent out of the sun and air have made her skin too sensitive. Tugging the rough fabric over her body is painful. She bites her lip until it bleeds.

Because she has nothing else she washes her face with her drinking water. Her broken fingernails must serve as a comb. She drags them through her tangled locks. It has been months since she paid attention to her hair. She is startled to discover the raven tresses are streaked with silver.

An armed guard takes her from the cell and leads her through a warren of passages. She tries to memorise the way in case she can break free. It is hopeless, however. Months of captivity have taken the strength from her legs. Besides, the guards have fastened shackles on her ankles as well as her hands. Even if she had the strength she could not run, only shuffle.

Granuaile is taken to a roughly plastered, low-ceilinged chamber with several windows set in one wall. In front of the windows stands a long oaken table. She can see very little because the light dazzles her eyes. She fears her sight may have been damaged by months of near-darkness.

One of her guards prods her in the back, pushing her forward. When she stumbles, someone laughs.

Squinting, she tries to make out the features of the person who faces her across the table. He gets to his feet as she approaches. He is a thickset man with pale eyes. Eyes as colourless as water in a cup.

To be a leader one must be a good judge of men. Granuaile has spent years reading the character of men from their faces. Lord Grey is newly arrived in Ireland, a place he has never visited before. His features are stern, but there is a certain watchfulness in his pale eyes that hints of uncertainty. He is a man who has yet to find his sea legs in a new situation.

I can do this, Granuaile tells herself with a sudden surge of confidence. *I can play this game.*

chapter twenty
winning the game

Granuaile meets twice with Lord Grey. He speaks neither Irish nor Spanish. Because she does not want him to know that she is educated, she speaks no Latin. *It is best if he underestimates me*, she thinks.

When she is first brought before him she jabbers very urgently in Irish, as if she has something important to tell. She waves her arms. She makes wild gestures. Then she catches his eyes and holds them. She begins to speak more slowly. She wants him to think she is being reasonable, even if he cannot understand her words.

An interpreter is soon provided. Granuaile twists her hands together and bows low in gratitude.

With no great difficulty she convinces the lord justice that she is a poor, sad old woman. In remorse for her crimes she pounds her breast with her fists. She bites her tongue to make tears come to her eyes.

Grey is very moved. When she begins to tear her hair out, he motions to one of his guards to hold her hands.

Then he comes around the table and strokes her shoulder to calm her.

The new lord justice is not as clever as he thinks. He judges Granuaile by what he sees. She tells herself, *he would not long survive at sea, where one must read the tides beneath the surface.*

Among the many rumours she has heard in the dungeons of Dublin Castle is one about Lord Grey. He is to lead the queen's armies in putting down the Desmond rebellion. Granuaile describes in detail the damage Desmond has done her. She stresses her passionate thirst for revenge. Then she makes an offer.

'If I am allowed to return to my ships,' she tells the lord justice, 'my fleet will prevent any supplies reaching Desmond by way of Limerick and the Shannon.'

Grey listens thoughtfully, then dismisses her. She is not taken back to her cell. Instead she is given a room elsewhere in the Castle, and the next morning he sends for her again. This time she is brought to him without shackles.

Granuaile knows then that she has won.

'Of course we cannot permit you to resume your piracy and raiding,' Grey tells her. 'Such deeds defy the queen's law.'

She keeps her face blank. Elizabeth Tudor is building a vast network through piracy and raiding, but she does not mention this.

She is fighting for her life. Sometimes that is best done with silence.

Lord Grey says, 'However, there is one way in which you can retain command of your fleet. If you use them only to deny supplies to the rebel Desmond, your ships will not be seized. Are we agreed?'

Granuaile bows low. Very low. 'Her Majesty is most generous,' she replies.

She does not actually give her word, however. She lets the lord justice think she has given her word, which is not the same thing. Granuaile is of the Gael – she will not break an oath once given. But never will she swear an oath to her enemies.

Having to go through an interpreter helps. Without a language in common, there is always the possibility of being misunderstood.

Grey believes what he wants to believe, as people do. Then he makes a generous gesture of his own. 'As the queen's obedient servant,' Grey tells her, 'you will be allowed to rest in Dublin for a few weeks to regain your strength. I shall arrange an apartment for you in an inn nearby. A small sum will be provided for your personal needs. You will be able to purchase food and wine and a few bits of clothing. When you are fit for the journey, you will be put aboard the next ship going to Galway.'

●　　　●　　　●

The following day, Granuaile smuggles out a note to her youngest son, now eleven years old:

My dear Toby,

Tell your father to have my men meet me with my favourite galley, but not in Galway. Send them to Bunowen to wait for me. And send them armed.

I am coming home.

Always,
Granuaile

chapter twenty-one
back to war

A feeble old woman totters off the English merchant ship onto the docks of Galway. Her shoulders are bowed, her head hangs low. The sailors watching from the deck elbow each other and laugh. They call out a few insults but she does not respond. Then they return to unloading their cargo. One more pitiful, broken prisoner is soon forgotten.

The sailors do not watch her walk away. They do not see her head gradually come up, her shoulders go back, her stride lengthen. The years fall away from her. By the time she reaches the city gates, Granuaile is once more the she-king of the western seas.

Granuaile meets with her sons Owen and Murrough at Bunowen, then goes to Achill Island to visit her daughter Margaret. Her children are startled by her changed appearance. 'There is no need to be concerned,' she tells them. 'Though my hair is grey and my face is gaunt, my heart is as strong as ever.'

90

When at last she sees Toby at Rockfleet she merely puts her arms around him and holds on tight.

⦿　⦿　⦿

After spending the summer at sea, Granuaile feels restored. The sea is both her home and her business. She rests on its bosom. She ploughs its waters as landmen plough their fields. Its fish are her herds. When she longs for companionship she listens to the voice of the waves.

The sea has been her teacher, too. There were times at sea when she has been hungry, thirsty, frightened, exhausted, too cold, too hot, and in great peril. Sometimes all in the same voyage. Surviving the hardships of a seagoing life has given Granuaile a quick mind and the ability to endure anything.

In the autumn the pope sends a small force of French, Spanish, and English troops to the southern coast of Ireland. Their purpose is to unite the Irish against the heretic Elizabeth. They are seeking help from the earl of Desmond among others. Although Desmond treated Granuaile badly, she decides to be his ally in the struggle.

'My enemy's enemy must be my friend,' she tells Richard Bourke.

There is much to do. Employing all her skills of secrecy, she begins importing guns for the princes of the north. The earl of Tyrone, Hugh O'Neill, and his ally Hugh O'Donnell are determined that Ulster will not be conquered.

Some of the O'Malleys and the O'Flaherties attempt to come to the aid of the pope's invasion force. They urge The MacWilliam to join them. He refuses, but Richard Bourke accepts. He leads a band of warriors to plunder territories known to be sympathetic to the English.

Although they do not live as man and wife any more, Granuaile is quietly proud of Richard-in-Iron.

Then Sir Nicholas Malby replaces Sir Edward Fitton as governor of Connacht. Malby seizes a castle belonging to Richard's chief counsellor. He puts its occupants – men, women and children alike – to the sword. This demonstration of deliberate cruelty frightens Richard's followers. They claim they must go home to help with the herds, to help with the harvest ... and they melt away. One after another, they melt away.

When Malby captures Burrishoole, Richard's defeat seems certain.

Granuaile tells him that making a voluntary submission is better than being taken prisoner on the battlefield. 'Tell them what they want to hear,' she says, 'and at least you will survive.'

But Richard has the bit in his teeth now. He does not play games, he insists, he is a warrior! He will fight to the death!

'And to the death of our son,' Granuaile retorts. 'If you continue in this reckless way, Tibbott will pay for it.' She orders her men to seize Richard and bundle him onto a ship to Scotland. There he is left to reflect on his position.

Some time later, when Granuaile learns that Shane MacOliverus is failing in health, she brings Richard back to Ireland. Although he grumbles, he does as Granuaile insists. Together they travel to Galway to offer his submission to Malby.

Granuaile stands at Richard's shoulder as he bows before the Englishman – but she does not bow. She listens as he makes promises of submission – but she does not speak.

Her eyes stare off into a far distance.

Malby is surprisingly pleasant to the pair of them. After the formalities are over he offers food and wine. He even compliments Richard on the exceptional energy of his wife.

Granuaile pretends not to understand, but when Malby smiles at her she briefly smiles back. He is only human after all.

In November of 1580, Shane MacOliverus dies. Over the objections of the dead man's younger brother, Malby allows Richard-in-Iron to assume the title of The MacWilliam.

The revolt in Mayo is over.

But Granuaile is still secretly running guns into Ulster for O'Donnell and O'Neill.

In September of 1581, Richard-in-Iron is granted a knighthood. Granuaile and young Tibbott attend the ceremony in Galway. She stands with her hand on her son's shoulder. Her face is set in a proud mask. People assume she is proud of Richard. In actuality she is thinking of the large number of muskets she has just managed to obtain for Hugh O'Neill, Earl of Tyrone.

Ireland is far from conquered.

There are many tides beneath the surface.

the princes of
the north

June, the Year of Our Lord 1582, Rockfleet

My dear Toby,

I understand that your foster-father, Myles MacEvilly, has made you his heir. Most Anglo-Normans do not make generous gestures without expecting to get something out of it for themselves.

You are fifteen now. Pay heed to what I tell you about the ways of the world, Toby. If you are willing to learn from my experience, you will never have to pay the price I have paid for wisdom.

Thanks to my help, Richard Bourke is now The MacWilliam. Myles MacEvilly needs The MacWilliam's support against an English officer who is trying to claim some of his holdings. By indicating his intention to leave his estate to you, MacEvilly obligates your father to protect it.

Protecting property under the new English law is not straightforward. In case of a dispute, one must prove right of ownership to the magistrates. If Richard's personal army is not enough to protect MacEvilly land, his title probably will be. English magistrates are more impressed by titles than by men.

I find this strange. An English title can be bought or sold or bartered like a bale of hides. If any man can own one, how can such a thing be valuable? Under Gaelic law a chieftain is elected by his people. Through his wise judgements, his generosity, or his military prowess, he earns the right to lead. Yet the English persuade foolish men to trade their Irish chieftaincies for English lordships.

Sometimes I despair for the future. We are too easily impressed. The foreigners appeal to our greed and offer us puffs of wind, while they steal our true gold from us.

We must outwit them, Toby. And we can.

Always,
Granuaile

● ● ●

Granuaile continues to sell her services to the princes of the north. She hopes the guns she brings into Ireland will help to break the grip of the foreigners. She would carry the weapons for free if necessary, although she does not say this to her clients.

The chieftains of Tyrconnell and Tyrone entertain her in their strongholds. One of O'Donnell's sons, a merry lad called Aed Rua, becomes her favourite. He is not as old as Toby, yet he is as brash and bold as a grown warrior, and his people love him dearly. Great things are predicted for Red Hugh.

Meanwhile Richard Bourke's family is at the height of its power. In Mayo, Granuaile appears in public at his side. She takes full advantage of the protective cloak her position as his wife offers. The English do not understand that she is an independent woman.

the death of
Richard-in-iron

The following year, Richard-in-Iron fights his last battle. It is a battle with illness, and one that he cannot win. Granuaile is more distressed by his death than she cares to admit. Many disliked him, but she has had no cause to complain of him. Once he realised that her judgement was better than his and consented to be guided by her, they had a smooth enough voyage together.

With Richard dead, there is fresh trouble. The English have named the younger brother of Shane MacOliverus as The MacWilliam. Some of the Bourkes will not accept MacOliverus as chieftain, because he was never tanaiste. Edmund Bourke of Castle Barry was Shane's chosen successor. The Bourkes split over the issue. With the English interfering, all Mayo may become a battlefield.

● ● ●

My dear Toby,

You are sixteen years old now, a grown man. Richard's stronghold at Burrishoole is part of your inheritance. I urge you to go there and take up residence at once. I feel confident that Malby will not object. Some of your Bourke kinsmen might, though. If necessary, I shall send for your O'Flaherty half-brothers to come up from Iar Connacht and help you defend your holding. Murrough is an aggressive man and always happy to fight. Owen is more peaceful of nature, but he can handle a sword or pistol well enough. I know, for I taught him.

I shall remain at Rockfleet. My favourite galley is moored at the foot of the tower. My men sleep in the banqueting hall and guard all the approaches. Anyone who attacks me here, English or Anglo-Norman, will regret it.

What I have I hold. Mind that you hold what is yours.

Always,

Granuaile

◉   ◉   ◉

The tall, lean woman prowls the battlements of Rockfleet. A rising wind whips her hair into her eyes. She tosses her head impatiently. Although she can smell ice on the wind and knows hail is coming, she prefers to be outside. She will not go in until the storm forces her to take shelter.

How different the tower seems, she thinks, *without Richard*. It had not been his home for years – during most of their marriage he lived at Burrishoole. Yet now that he is gone, Granuaile senses him on the stair, in the armoury, in the great hall. Sometimes in the night she hears him snoring in bed beside her. When she jumps up and lights a candle, no one is there.

No one is ever there. Only her memories.

Her memories stalk the battlements of Rockfleet Castle.

A shiver runs up her spine. The rain has not begun, but Granuaile is cold. She makes the sign of the cross on her breast and turns to go inside.

Against her expectations, Mayo remains at peace. The battles that raged over the chieftainship are over. The brother of Shane MacOliverus holds the title. Cathair-na-Mart was burnt to the ground and Granuaile's half-brother Donal is homeless, but at least he is still alive. When he whines, she reminds him that he has much to be thankful for.

'Being alive is no small thing,' she tells him. 'I hate a man who snivels even more than I hate a coward. There is some excuse for fear. There is never any excuse for whining. A man who pities himself has no pity left over for others.'

Granuaile fears they may all soon need pity. Malby has died, and his successor as governor of Connacht is Richard Bingham, a man she knows only by reputation. Bingham has stated publicly that the Irish are vermin.

The campaign to conquer Desmond has proved very expensive for the English. They finally succeeded, but only by devastating Munster with fire and famine. If Bingham has his way, Connacht will receive the same treatment.

Meanwhile Sir John Perrot has succeeded Lord Grey as lord deputy of Ireland. Unlike Bingham, Perrot is said to be a moderate man. He believes persuasion is preferable to armed force. Therefore the policy of 'Surrender and Regrant' is being urged upon the Irish chieftains. If they surrender their holdings and their claims to an Irish title, they are granted new English titles. They are also given back some, though not all, of the lands they formerly held.

The English ignore the fact that this land was held in common for the chieftain's clan. It was never his personal property to barter away.

They are tricking us into selling the very earth beneath our feet! Granuaile fumes. *The earth that holds our fathers' fathers. But they cannot buy the sea.*

The sea is mine.

stealing tibbott

A new document is drawn up by Perrot's officials. Called 'The Composition of Connacht', it reflects sweeping changes in the possession of land. The ancient clanholds are carved up and lost. Chieftains who resist are slain and their holdings seized anyway. Perrot may be moderate compared to Richard Bingham, but his policies are destroying Gaelic Ireland.

Granuaile continues to sail with her fleet. Although she is careful to avoid English warships, her trade and piracy go on as before. This is the tradition she inherited. She cannot imagine any other way of living.

Granuaile's name turns up with increasing frequency in reports to the new governor of Connacht. At first Bingham does not take the matter seriously. A woman? She cannot be much of a threat. Then he learns that she is importing guns into Ulster. Worse still, she is harassing merchant ships along the coast. Valuable trade is being lost.

Bingham has secretly arranged for a percentage of all trade in western waters to find its way to his own purse.

He sets himself to learn as much as he can about the notorious pirate queen. One of the facts he discovers is the existence of her youngest son, Tibbott Bourke. By all reports Tibbott is the blood in his mother's heart.

In July of 1584, while Granuaile is overseeing a refitting of her favourite galley, a messenger arrives on Clare Island. 'Richard Bingham has taken your son Tibbott prisoner!' he blurts out.

She stares at him in horror. 'Are you certain?'

'I am one of Tibbott's servants. I was there when they seized him and carried him away in a cart.'

Granuaile leaps to her feet and begins to stride back and forth across the room, striking the palm of one hand with the fist of the other. The messenger is terrified by the expression on her face. 'I would have saved him if I could!' he tells her repeatedly.

Granuaile does not hear him. She is muttering to herself. 'Bingham commanded me to cease my seafaring operations, but I would not. With Toby as a hostage he thinks he can force me to submit to his will.'

Suddenly she throws up her head and fixes the frightened messenger with a fierce glare. 'Where have they taken my son, do you know?'

'I overheard the orders being given. He was to be delivered to Richard Bingham's brother George, at Ballymote Castle in Sligo.'

Granuaile nods. 'I know the place. It is well fortified, we cannot hope to break him out of there. But perhaps we can get a message to him. Can I trust you?'

'Are you not Granuaile?' the man replies. 'You can trust me with your life, for I would give mine for your sake.'

She hastily writes a letter to Tibbott, asking the exact circumstances of his confinement. She waits with impatience for an answer. When it comes Granuaile tears off the seal of red wax and devours the words with her eyes.

Toby writes that he is comfortable and being treated well. 'Like one of the family,' he explains. 'I have my own quarters and am allowed the freedom of the house.'

Granuaile folds his letter and taps it against her teeth as she stares into space.

We are presented with an opportunity here, she tells herself. *Even disasters can be turned to profit if one is clever.* She reaches for pen and paper.

●　　●　　●

August, the Year of Our Lord 1584, Clare Island

My dear Toby,

While you are in Bingham's household, you must learn to read and write English. Elizabeth's administrators want everything bound up in documents. I need someone who can understand their language. Someone to be my spy within the enemy's walls.

You will be free in time, I swear it. Meanwhile, do whatever is necessary to keep yourself safe. For my sake. It is far from where you were born that life takes you, so adjust your sails to the wind.

Always,

Granuaile

● ● ●

She writes calmly and reassuringly to her son, but inside she is frantic. *Bingham has Toby. Dear God, he has Toby!*

With an aching heart, she gives the order for her fleet to be beached indefinitely.

The winter comes early this year, and lasts long. Cold winds howl around the tower of Rockfleet. Granuaile stays inside most of the time. She cannot bear the sight of the empty bay.

She is not defeated, though. She is merely waiting.

chapter twenty-five

summoned

In June of 1585, Richard Bingham summons the Mayo chieftains to Galway. The summons also includes Granuaile, to her surprise. She has been beseeching him for months to discuss the matter of her son's captivity, but until now he has ignored her. It is a cruel and deliberate torture.

When she arrives in Galway Granuaile does not know what to expect. So many dreadful tales are being told of Bingham. And as soon as she sees him, she knows the stories are true. Richard Bingham has a long, cold, sharp-featured face, his dark beard tightly trimmed in the English fashion. He reminds Granuaile of a weasel. A weasel dressed in a velvet doublet and a high collar.

In the large chamber that serves as his audience room, he moves down the line of assembled chieftains while his secretary calls each person by name. Bingham speaks to a few, hardly glances at others. But when he reaches Granuaile, their eyes meet. Lock. Something passes between them.

Occasionally, when two strange hounds meet in the road, the hackles rise on their necks. Even though they have never seen each other before, they bare their fangs and stiffen their forelegs. They will fight to the death if someone does not pull them apart.

That is what happens between Granuaile and Richard Bingham.

She tries to hide her emotions. 'I hoped you would have my son with you,' she says politely. 'It would have been proper to include Tibbott among the Mayo chieftains, as his father's heir.'

Bingham smiles, revealing narrow yellow teeth. 'You were hoping to help him escape,' he replies shrewdly. Abruptly he snaps his fingers. His secretary begins reading from a list that contains the names of the chieftains who have accepted Surrender and Regrant. 'Warrants will be issued for those who have refused,' Bingham announces, 'and for those who are absent. It is assumed they are traitors. Their deaths will be sought.'

Granuaile gasps. 'My son …'

'Ah yes. Your son. First let us discuss your situation, Grace O'Malley. If you are willing to be agreeable, you will be allowed to live out your life undisturbed. You may even attend Tibbott Bourke's wedding.'

Her jaw drops. 'What?'

'Tibbott has been writing to you, I understand. Has he not told you of his betrothal?' Bingham is enjoying this enormously. 'My brother George introduced your son to Maude O'Connor of Sligo, and now they are to be married.

Is that not happy news? She is a fine young woman of unquestioned loyalty to the Queen, and your son is an intelligent man. Through this marriage our two peoples will develop new bonds of ... friendship.' Bingham smiles again. The smile of a weasel just before it kills.

Granuaile is struggling to understand. The Sligo O'Connors are a prominent Irish family who have accepted the dominance of the English. They have even changed the name of their daughter Maeve to Maude. *And this is the young woman Toby will marry*, Granuaile thinks. *Through her, Bingham binds my son with a silken web. To control me. It is all done to control me. Men like Bingham use women as pawns.*

But I am not like other women and the game is not over yet, no matter what Bingham thinks.

chapter twenty-six

the devil's hook

Although Owen and Murrough O'Flaherty are mentioned in the Composition of Connacht, these two sons of Granuaile have not signed the document. They refuse to acknowledge that the English have any right to redistribute Irish lands. The same is true for many of the Bourkes of Mayo. Even those who originally signed are beginning to regret their actions.

Throughout her life Granuaile has known when a storm was brewing, even before the first puff of wind. Her oldest son, Owen, is married to Edmund Bourke's daughter. Granuaile sends him a message urging him to be cautious. 'Give Bingham no reason to connect you with me,' she suggests.

With his wife and dependents, Owen O'Flaherty withdraws to Ballinahinch Castle. At the end of January 1586, Richard Bingham hangs seventy members of the Bourke clan. But in the fastnesses of Iar Connacht, Granuaile's oldest son is left at peace.

The following month The MacWilliam dies. Once again the English authorities fail to accept Edmund Bourke as the new chieftain, though many of the Bourkes regard him as the rightful heir. Although he is an old man, Edmund Bourke rebels. His rebellion is supported by his kinsman, The Devil's Hook, who is married to Granuaile's daughter Margaret. The Bourkes fight hard, but by March they are forced to retreat to an island stronghold in Lough Mask.

The Devil's Hook sends to Granuaile for help.

When the message reaches Rockfleet she goes out onto the battlements and gazes across the bay toward Croagh Patrick. Richard is gone, Tibbott is far away. She has no one to confide in but God ... and the holy mountain.

'I have let Bingham frighten me for too long,' she cries aloud, 'and I hate being frightened. Enough is enough!' Granuaile's voice echoes across the expanse of blue water. 'Enough is enough! Enough is enough!'

Sending for her personal boatmen, she sets out across the bay to Clare Island. There she orders her galleys back into the water.

Her fleet reaches Lough Mask as Richard Bingham is besieging the island. The sound of musket fire makes her blood simmer with excitement. It is like the old days again. Bingham is commanding several boats laden with warriors, but Granuaile has the advantage of more agile craft. Sweeping across the lake, she drives the English away from the island. The boat containing Bingham is overturned and he is nearly drowned.

His men raise a great cry that identifies him. Granuaile peers over the rail of her own galley. She thinks she sees a dark head bobbing in the water. 'Shoot him!' she shouts to her musketeers. 'Blow him to bits!'

But musket fire is unreliable at best. At a distance, trying to hit a tiny target in a choppy lake, there is little hope of success.

Bingham is a strong swimmer. He makes it to shore, where a party of horsemen is waiting. 'He will send for reinforcements,' Granuaile warns her crew. 'We must get my son-in-law off the island before we find ourselves badly outnumbered.'

They anchor in the shallows and help The Devil's Hook and the others aboard. Then they set sail for Clew Bay. There are a hundred secret places in that vast wilderness of islands, where fugitives can hide and never be found.

Richard Bingham cannot admit that he has been outdone. He begins hanging those members of the Bourke clan within his reach – even those who have submitted to him and took no part in the revolt.

Tibbott Bourke seems safe enough, however. His personal connection with George Bingham offers protection. He is even allowed to take his new wife back to Burrishoole.

Her success against Richard Bingham has strengthened Granuaile's confidence. It is a small victory and has cost lives, but at least she was not beaten.

She was not beaten. She hugs this knowledge to her breast.

● ● ●

She has not long to enjoy her triumph.

In June, unfamiliar ships sail into the mouth of Clew Bay. Granuaile goes out in her curragh to demand they pay the traditional fee for entering her waters. She does not realise that another brother of Richard Bingham captains the vessels. He has come to Mayo in search of plunder. When he sees the tall, swarthy woman who dresses like a man and challenges him in a hoarse voice, John Bingham knows exactly who she is.

At first he appears willing to negotiate with her. But it is a trick. As soon as he has Granuaile on his flagship, John Bingham gives an order for his crew to seize her. Then he sends his men ashore to take her cattle and horses.

While Granuaile was in prison her people had depended on those herds for survival. Now she has to stand on the deck, bound hand and foot, and watch while her walking wealth is driven aboard English ships.

She can hear the cattle bawling as John Bingham gives the order to weigh anchor and set sail.

● ● ●

July, the Year of Our Lord 1586, Rockfleet

My dear Toby,

I have been cruelly tricked. John Bingham stole my livestock and took me to Galway, where he turned me over to his brother. The governor refused to hear my complaints about being robbed of my property. I was treated as a common criminal and thrown into a cell.

Being imprisoned again was more than I could bear. I confess to you, my son, that I could feel madness run toward me with the scampering rats.

I could hear hammering in the courtyard. 'They are building a gallows especially for you,' my gaolers told me.

Then a miracle occurred. I had risked myself to save The Devil's Hook at Lough Mask. So he surrendered himself to Richard Bingham in return for my freedom. He will stand hostage to ensure my good conduct.

That is what it means to be part of a clan, Toby. We are tied with bonds stouter than rope. The man who married my daughter is my son as surely as if I had given birth to him. How can anyone break us!

Even Richard Bingham was impressed by the gesture. He took my son-in-law into custody for a twelvemonth. Before he would let me go, however, the governor demanded that I give up my seafaring enterprises. Yet he kept my herds. He said I owed them to the queen to pay for my past crimes.

Without cattle I have no way to support myself and my people, but the sea.

I am not held by chains and bars, yet Bingham has me in a prison just the same. He cannot hold me, though. I will find a way to be free.

Always,
Granuaile

chapter twenty-seven
feeding the enemy

Richard Bingham is not through with the Bourkes. Once he has The Devil's Hook in Galway Gaol, he sets out to destroy the remaining resistance. Edmund Bourke is ninety years of age and still defiant. But without The Devil's Hook to protect him, he is captured. At the end of July the governor hangs the old man.

Then Richard Bingham appoints his brother John as his lieutenant in Iar Connacht. With five hundred men, John Bingham marches to Ballinahinch Castle. When he arrives Bingham demands hospitality of Owen O'Flaherty.

O'Flaherty has no choice but to feed his enemy.

The New English have overthrown Gaelic law, yet still it binds the oldest son of Granuaile.

Granuaile had thought being in prison was the worst thing that could happen to her. It is not.

John Bingham and his men eat her son's bread and salt in Ballinahinch Castle, then seize Owen. They also take his family and servants captive. With none to hinder them, they steal his cattle and horses and all his personal property. They even take the reliquary from the family chapel.

The English hang Owen's men without any pretence of giving them a trial first. They even hang a helpless old fellow who had the misfortune to be a guest in the castle when Bingham arrived. The womenfolk are herded together into one of the outbuildings and left alone in the dark.

Owen is imprisoned in a bedchamber with a heavy bar across the door. A guard is stationed outside. John Bingham is careful to say, in front of witnesses, that he means Owen O'Flaherty to be kept safe from harm.

Sometime during the night voices call from outside the castle, warning that an attack is underway. The guard at Owen's chamber leaves his post to see what is happening. It proves to be a false alarm. When he returns the door is still barred, or so he claims. But when it is opened in the morning, Owen O'Flaherty lies dead within the room. Blood is still seeping from at least twelve wounds.

John Bingham claims to know nothing about the murder. He turns the women loose to mourn, packs up his stolen booty, and rides away laughing.

Granuaile had thought she knew every sort of pain, but this is a new one. *Owen. First born, first lost.*

The murder of her son is bad enough. Almost worse is the feeling that she failed him. When he was growing up she spent most of her time at sea. She had thought to provide her children with a secure future by making their clan prosperous, but that was a false hope. Security, she knows now, is an illusion.

Owen is forever beyond his mother's reach. She cannot make anything up to him. Or to his brother Murrough, for that matter. Bitter and angry, Murrough goes his own way. He will not listen to Granuaile. He blames her for making an enemy of the Binghams.

Sidney, Malby, even Lord Grey, treated Granuaile as something of a curiosity. They used her as a pawn, but they were generous enough when it suited them. The Binghams are different. They seem determined to destroy her personally.

Restless as a tiger, she prowls the invisible boundaries of her cage. She can take a currach to Achill to see her daughter Margaret, or even sail one of her galleys back and forth across Clew Bay. But not outside. Not onto the broad lap of the open sea.

chapter twenty-eight
plots and plans

May, the Year of Our Lord 1587, Donegal

My dear Toby,

Do not be surprised when you learn where I am. For the moment at least I have slipped Bingham's clutches.

As you may know, The Devil's Hook escaped from Galway Gaol. When he appeared at Achill I was glad for my daughter's sake, but I knew what it meant for me. My son-in-law had been my pledge of good conduct. Now that he was free, Bingham would drag me back to prison – or the gallows.

Under cover of a dense fog, I slipped out of Clew Bay with my three best galleys. I was determined to make a run for the north. As we entered Sligo Bay a terrible storm blew up. Rarely have I met such a gale. Again and again, we were blown toward the rocks. All my seamanship, and my crew's courage, was needed to keep us afloat. By the time we reached safe harbour in Donegal my ships were battered almost to pieces. But we were beyond the reach of the governor of Connacht.

It is wonderful to be among allies.

Hugh Dubh O'Donnell has invited me to stay in Donegal Castle for as long as I like. It will take many weeks to repair my ships to the standard I demand. They were built to my order in La Coruña, in Spain, and there is no one here with similar skills.

I shall pass the time by conferring with the princes of Ulster. Hugh O'Neill will be coming here within the next few weeks from his stronghold at Dungannon. He wants to discuss the rumours of a possible Spanish invasion of England. Spain is a Catholic country, like Ireland. King Philip of Spain desires to see Catholicism restored in England. He is also very angry about English piracy against Spanish trade and possessions.

If Philip attacks Elizabeth we will ally ourselves with the Spanish. Together we can break the hold of England on this island once and for all.

O'Donnell's son, Red Hugh, is wildly excited by the prospect. The young lad is ready to take up arms tomorrow. I remember when I was like that. The blood ran hot in my veins and I thought I was immortal. Red Hugh makes me feel that way again.

Always,
Granuaile

Hugh O'Neill, Earl of Tyrone, arrives in Tyrconnell with all the trappings of the Gaelic nobility. O'Neill is considerably younger than O'Donnell. He is a sturdy, handsome man in the prime of life. His followers are devoted to him. He is considered the foremost chieftain of the north, although he speaks Irish with a peculiarly English accent.

The poverty that is so visible elsewhere, as the English strip the island of its resources, has not reached this part of the country. The north is still the land of the Gael. For size and luxury Donegal Castle rivals any in Ireland, and O'Donnell entertains his guests lavishly. In the great hall storytellers repeat the ancient hero-tales to a spellbound audience. Harpers play familiar airs on beautifully carved instruments. A whole ox roasts over a fire that hisses and snaps as the fat drips onto the coals. Children are given bowls of Ulster apples swimming in honey and cream.

The wine runs red.

Red. Like blood. A vision of her murdered son Owen flickers through Granuaile's brain and she shudders.

She leans forward, propping her elbows on the table. 'What news of the Spanish invasion?' she asks in a low, urgent voice.

'Nothing yet,' O'Neill tells her.

She slumps back on her bench.

During the day she goes down to the harbour to supervise the repairs to her ships. Night after night, she joins O'Neill and O'Donnell to discuss the political situation. Other women talk of their husbands and children, but Granuaile does not spend her time with other women.

In spite of the ongoing discussions about rebellion, the north remains peaceful. O'Donnell and O'Neill are thoughtful men. They agree to wait and see what the Spanish do before they act.

Passing seamen report that Mayo is at peace as well. In July Elizabeth sends Richard Bingham to Flanders as a reward for his services. The search for Granuaile is abandoned as the new governor finds all his time is taken up with the administration of the province.

'It is time I went home,' Granuaile says. Her friends assure her that she is welcome to spend the rest of her life with one of them. 'How much can one old woman eat?' Hugh O'Neill laughs.

Granuaile is not amused. She is not ready to be an old woman, living on the hospitality of her friends. At night she dreams of Clew Bay. She can almost hear the cries of the kittiwakes, almost see people waving from the shore of Clare Island.

'I have a letter from my son Tibbott,' she tells O'Donnell, 'and I have to go home.'

'Why? Are the English threatening him?'

Granuaile shakes her head. 'Tibbott does not fear the English. In his youth he was a hostage in the household of George Bingham, and formed relationships which have kept him safe ever since.'

Hugh O'Neill says, 'Elizabeth Tudor wants the sons of Irish chieftains to be converted into obedient English subjects. When I was nine years old Sir Henry Sidney took me to England. His family dressed 'their little Irish savage' in velvets and laces and taught me manners. Elizabeth Tudor treated me as her special pet,' he adds with a curl of his lip. 'She was fond of me and gave me many gifts. I made a number of friends at court. Friends I retain to this day. Then, when I was seventeen and a man, Elizabeth sent me back to Ireland as earl of Tyrone.'

'Yet I assure you, Granuaile – if the queen knew I was plotting against her now, she would hate me more than if I had been her enemy from the start.'

chapter twenty-nine

the capture of red hugh

Granuaile is glad to be back in Rockfleet, but she does not sleep well. Her bed has grown damp in her absence. In the morning she spreads her linen sheets on the parapet to dry in the wind. Although it is late summer, she also builds a fire in the bedchamber.

As she stands watching the flames, she wonders if there is any timber at Burrishoole. The English are sending tons of oak back to England for shipbuilding. The woodlands beyond Belclare are almost destroyed.

It is important, Granuaile thinks, *that Toby has enough timber to keep the fires going this winter, now that he and Maude are expecting a child.*

She invites her son to Rockfleet to discuss the future.

When Toby arrives, Granuaille tells him about the rebellion of the princes of Ulster. Toby's immediate reaction is concern for his own property. He has been granted Burrishoole by the English. If his mother is involved in a conspiracy he could lose everything. 'Everything you wanted for me!' he reminds her.

Granuaile cannot help comparing her son to young Red Hugh O'Donnell. Tibbott's gaze is guarded. He speaks slowly, weighing every word.

I have made him too cautious, Granuaile thinks sadly. *In my eagerness to keep him safe I have crippled his spirit. In my heart I really want a son like Red Hugh. That dauntless boy ... I wish I had the prince of Donegal here in Connacht. Together we could drive the English out.*

Tibbott sees his mother's attention wandering. She is getting old, he believes. Soon she will forget this dangerous nonsense about rebelling.

'What are you thinking about?' he asks.

Granuaile merely smiles.

In the autumn of 1587, the lord deputy, Sir John Perrot, is ordered to extend English control into Tyrconnell. He demands that O'Donnell give him hostages of good conduct. When the old man refuses, Perrot sends a merchant ship to Tyrconnell, ostensibly loaded with French wine for Donegal Castle. Red Hugh is invited on board to inspect the merchandise before it is delivered. The young prince accepts the invitation and brings three of his friends.

They are seized by the English and put in chains. The ship promptly weighs anchor and makes for Dublin.

The Eagle of the North, the bold lad with a merry laugh and hair like flame, is caged in Dublin Castle.

Hugh Dubh O'Donnell does all he can to recover his son. He writes letter after letter to Perrot, who forwards them to London. But Elizabeth's privy council decides the young prince is too valuable to be released.

Red Hugh remains in Dublin Castle. He is not even permitted to send a letter to his father.

O'Donnell's attitude hardens. He begins preparing for rebellion and orders his Scots mercenaries into the field. For the sake of his son he is willing to bathe Ireland in blood.

❀   ❀   ❀

January, the Year of Our Lord 1588, Rockfleet

My dear Toby,

Your education in the English language will be of benefit now. Compose a letter for me, addressed to Sir John Perrot. Use the words and phrases the English like. Sound humble, respectful. Ask for a full pardon for myself and my family. That is important. Stress that the pardon is to include you and your children as well. I shall carry the request to Dublin and personally present it to the lord deputy. I know Perrot. If I can meet him face to face again, I believe I can persuade him.

I have no fear for myself but you are bringing new life into the world, and new life must be protected.

Always,
Granuaile

Granuaile makes the journey to Dublin in one galley, with no fleet at her back. She does not want to look dangerous. She goes as a helpless old woman, pleading.

With gritted teeth.

a pardon from perrot

The bright blue skies of June arch over the deep blue waters of Clew Bay. A single galley, with the flag of the white seahorse, is making for Clare Island.

The woman who stands tall in the prow is returning home. Her weather-lined face is a study in mixed emotions: triumph and anxiety.

Granuaile is carrying a letter signed by Sir John Perrot and dated 4 May, 1588. On behalf of Elizabeth of England, the document pardons Granuaile and her family for all past misdeeds, except murder, debt or intrusion on land belonging to the Crown. The royal pardon comes too late for Owen, but Murrough, Margaret and Toby should be safe from the fate that has befallen Red Hugh O'Donnell. This is Granuaile's triumph.

The source of her anxiety is the news she brings. As her followers crowd around her, she tells them what she learned in Dublin. 'King Philip of Spain has undertaken the invasion of England. A great armada, estimated as almost two hundred ships, has set sail from Lisbon. The

English fear the Spanish may use Ireland as a staging point, or at least seek to re-supply themselves there. Therefore Elizabeth is sending Richard Bingham back to Connacht to deal with the threat. Even as I speak to you, he is on his way to Galway.

'Bingham's return is a disaster. As you know from past experience, the man is exceptionally arrogant and cruel. Even Perrot was glad when Bingham went to Flanders. Now he returns. I have no doubt he will come after me. He may respect the queen's pardon in relation to the rest of my family, but not to me. The battle between Richard Bingham and myself will not be over until one of us dies.

'We must expect an attack on Umhall Ui Mhaille,' she warns. 'Fight with guns or swords or spears or bare hands, but fight. Do not surrender one more cow, one more horse, one more clod of earth, to the English!

'As for me, I will not allow Bingham to trap me and seize my ships.' Granuaile doubles her hands into fists. Her eyes blaze. 'If necessary I shall burn the galleys myself, keeping out one so I can make a break for freedom.'

chapter thirty-one

the spanish armada

The Spanish Armada is met with a stiff defence in the English Channel. Elizabeth's warships carry fewer men, but they are lighter and faster and their artillery is better. They do considerable damage to the clumsy Spanish vessels, but cannot overcome them. Gales in the Channel finally force the invaders back to Northern Spain, where they refit their ships.

In July the Armada sets forth again.

English and Dutch warships are waiting for the invaders at the mouth of the Channel. They launch fireships into the heart of the Spanish fleet, breaking its formation. In the battle that follows, a number of Spanish ships are sunk, damaged or scattered among the Channel Islands. The English harry them like hounds. The Spaniards are in danger of being driven aground. All hope of victory is lost. They try to escape, but the combination of pursuing warships and a strong wind forces them to sail north up the Channel, rather than south.

The English are forced to turn back by a shortage of supplies. What remains of the Armada reaches clear water in the North Sea. They round northern Scotland and chart a course down the west coast of Ireland, heading wearily home.

Meanwhile a huge storm has been brewing in the Atlantic. When the fleeing ships reach the west coast of Ireland they are battered by terrible winds. They struggle on. Their sails are torn from the masts. Helpless, they are driven onto the rocks. As the bulky warships break up, their timbers cry out like dying animals.

Aristocratic Spanish officers and common seamen are plunged together into the violent ocean. Those who can, swim desperately for shore.

⊛　　⊛　　⊛

September, the Year of Our Lord 1588, Achill Island

My dear Toby,

Disaster! All is undone. The Spanish fleet has been destroyed, and only a few will ever reach their home port. I fear Spanish support for Ireland's cause is lost as well. Why? Because as the survivors from the wrecked Armada came ashore, we slaughtered them.

We had been watching the coast in anticipation of an attack by Bingham. When the storm blew up we could see ships battling against the wind. By their shape I knew them for Spanish, not English. I tried to tell people this but they would not listen. I cannot say what took hold of their minds. They went wild with excitement. They leaped up and down, screaming and waving their arms about as they watched the ships break up on the rocks.

There is no excuse for what they did next.

As the half-drowned Spaniards came staggering out of the sea, men, women and even children waded into the surf to take hold of them. The unfortunates were stripped of whatever valuables they carried, then battered to death there on the shore.

I ran up and down the beach, screaming at people to stop. They had never failed to obey me before. But in that howling wind, they were howling too. They were deaf and blind to everything but violence.

Is this what Bingham and his kind have done to us? Have they made us so fearful and frantic we kill without reason?

We have slain those who should be our allies, Toby. If word of this gets back to Philip, what help can we expect from him? We will be left alone against the English. But whilst there is life left in us, we must fight to keep go on living.

Always,
Granuaile

● ● ●

Heartsick, Granuaile prowls a coast littered with broken ships' timbers and dead bodies.

Her son-in-law, The Devil's Hook, has managed to rescue a few of the Spaniards. He has given them refuge in his stronghold on Achill Island. But between six and eight thousand men have died on the shores of Connacht.

Half buried in the sand, Granuaile finds an elegant dagger with fine gold wire wrapped around the hilt. It has just been uncovered by the receding tide. Granuaile stoops to pick it up. An officer's weapon, most likely. For all its beauty, the weapon shows signs of hard use. When Granuaile holds the weapon up to the sun, the blade does not gleam. It is badly nicked and covered with dark stains. The stains are not rust.

The Spanish have given me something after all, she thinks. She thrusts the dagger into her belt.

Word comes from Ulster. Clan O'Donnell has rescued a number of Armada survivors from ships wrecked off the coast of Donegal. They have been fed and clothed, and their injuries tended. But they are not yet on their way home. The O'Donnell has surrendered thirty Spanish officers to the English, pleading for the release of Red Hugh in return.

Once again Elizabeth's privy council refuses the request. They also replace Sir John Perrot with a new lord deputy for Ireland, a man called Sir William Fitzwilliam. He promises not to be so 'generous' with the Irish. Bingham's way of dealing with them suits him very well.

Richard Bingham orders that any Spaniards caught on the west coast are to be hanged at Galway. So are those who give them shelter.

When she learns of this Granuaile goes to warn The Devil's Hook, who has added the Spanish men he rescued to his own warrior band. 'Bingham will kill you if he finds out,' she tells her son-in-law.

'He will find out nothing,' The Devil's Hook reassures her. 'My people are totally loyal to me, as yours are to you. The Spaniards are safe with us. I can protect you as well. Why do you not stay here for a while and enjoy your grandchildren?'

The invitation is impossible to refuse. Granuaile feels old age creeping into her joints like mildew. She wants nothing more than to sit by the fire and let her grandchildren play around her feet.

Bingham takes an army into Ulster to put down rebellion there. Fitzwilliam, the new lord deputy, considers any Scottish presence in the north as dangerous. Bingham orders that all Scottish gallowglasses are to be shot on sight.

Granuaile brought most of those men to Ireland in her galleys. She prays that she has not delivered them to their deaths.

While Bingham savages the north, his policies in Connacht are enforced by his sheriffs. Hangings, torture, unfair taxes, land seizures – they can only have one result. Connacht will rebel too.

'So be it,' says Granuaile grimly. 'Let us see how many fires Richard Bingham can put out at once.'

On a bitterly cold January morning, signal fires blaze around the rim of Clew Bay. In his stronghold at Curraun, The Devil's Hook makes preparations.

The English-born sheriff of Mayo, John Browne, has recently received a message from Richard Bingham, ordering him to take the notorious Granuaile into custody. The sheriff's informers tell him that she is with her son-in-law on Achill Island.

But Granuaile has informers of her own. She knows Browne's intention before he sets out from Galway. Quietly, in the night, she leaves Achill and returns to Rockfleet.

Next day the signal fires report Browne's approach. The Devil's Hook is waiting for him on Achill Island.

The sheriff and his men are slain on the strand at Curraun.

Their blood seeps into the soil of Ireland.

chapter thirty-two

nurse to all rebellions

February, the Year of Our Lord 1589, Rockfleet

My dear Toby,

The rebellion I expected has begun. Almost every clan in Connacht is supplying warriors. If I were a little younger I would be in the forefront of the battle with a pistol in my hand. At least I can use my fleet as a weapon. My ships are transporting fighting men up and down the coast, wherever needed.

Examine your stores, my son. Be certain you have enough food to last for at least six weeks if you are besieged. Although there is a good spring at Burrishoole, order your servants to fill every container with fresh water as well.

Your armoury is well stocked with the muskets and pistols I imported. Inspect them thoroughly. Be certain each one is in working condition in case you are attacked.

When Bingham returns to Connacht he will find that we have repaid him in full measure for his cruelty. He has sown seeds of hatred. From them grows a tree of fire and fury.

Always,

Granuaile

⦿ ⦿ ⦿

The rebellion that erupts in Connacht alarms the new lord deputy. He had been assured that the province was submissive. This will not look good on his record. Soon the rebels hold not only Mayo but also parts of Sligo, Roscommon and Galway.

Fitzwilliam, the lord deputy, orders Richard Bingham to arrange a truce. Reluctantly, Bingham does so.

The Bourkes refuse to accept the truce. Advised by Granuaile, they demand that Richard Bingham be removed as governor of Connacht. A Book of Complaints against him is drawn up. He is charged with many acts of extreme cruelty.

Accompanied by Tibbott, Granuaile sails to Dublin to present the Book of Complaints to Fitzwilliam. The tall woman who strides into the lord deputy's chambers brings with her the scent of the sea. Her face might have been carved from the oaks of Ireland. Fitzwilliam's attendants shrink away from her as from a wild animal.

Fitzwilliam personally takes the book from Granuaile's hands. 'Her Majesty and I appreciate your informing us of Richard Bingham's ... shortcomings,' he says through an interpreter.

'Richard Bingham is a monster,' Granuaile replies flatly. 'Hang him.'

Then she and Tibbott go on to Scotland – to import more gallowglasses.

The queen's privy council orders Fitzwilliam to determine if Richard Bingham is guilty of the charges brought against him. Various witnesses, all carefully selected, give statements to the lord deputy. Bingham is cleared. In January of 1590 he is instructed to put down the rebellion by any means necessary. No measure is too severe

Bingham and his soldiers pursue a scorched earth policy. Rebel families are put to the sword and their homes and property destroyed. Irish men and women who have taken no part in the rebellion suffer the same fate. This turns them against the rebels, whom they blame for their misfortune. Even the most valiant Irish warriors cannot fight both the English and their own people.

By the end of March the rebellion is over.

To Granuaile's disgust, she learns that her second son, Murrough O'Flaherty, took the field on Bingham's side during the rebellion. For some time she refuses to believe this, but many people saw him. 'I do not know whether my son acted out of cowardice, or out of malice toward me,' she tells her followers.

The result is the same either way. She must respond.

Taking several galleys, she sets sail for Bunowen. Murrough returns from a cattle fair just in time to find his mother with a torch in her hands, burning one of his outbuildings. 'If I cannot defeat Richard Bingham,' she shouts at him, 'at least I can teach my own flesh and blood not to defy his mother!'

She is no longer the mother Murrough remembers. He hardly recognises her, this savage creature who is ordering her men to plunder his lands. If she were anyone else he would fight back. But something stops him.

Murrough O'Flaherty is afraid of Granuaile.

❋　　　❋　　　❋

Connacht can now be described as submissive once more, and Fitzwilliam can boast that he has pacified most of Ireland. Pockets of resistance keep appearing, and battles are fought here and there with mixed results, but the wild Irish have been brought to heel, the lord deputy assures Elizabeth.

Richard Bingham does not believe for a moment that his troubles with Granuaile are over. He is well aware that she possesses a pardon in the queen's name. She has very carefully not broken the provisions of the pardon. Although Granuaile's fleet was sailing up and down the coast during the rebellion, she herself did not take part in any fighting. She did not trespass on Crown property. She murdered no one.

The only attack she has led has been on her own son.

Bingham dare not hang her. His actions as governor of the province will be closely watched from now on. He cannot risk another Book of Complaints.

Sourly, Bingham writes of Granuaile, 'She is a notable traitoress and nurse to all rebellions in the province for forty years.'

chapter thirty-three

the hound's jaws

My dear Toby,

Richard Bingham is doing all he can to destroy me without laying hands on me. Bit by bit, he has reduced those I hold dear to poverty – except yourself. I have just learned that my daughter Margaret and her husband have hardly more than forty cows. Forty cows is a goodly number on Achill Island, but if the winter is a hard one, or if Bingham sends more soldiers seeking provisions, they could find themselves without meat. He would not hesitate to take away the last of their herds.

As long as I have my galleys, they will not starve. Even the ships are in danger, though. Bingham has given orders that no one in Galway is to sell me material for repairing them. Here in Mayo there is no leather for the curraghs, no timber for the galleys. The last of our forests were burned by the English to prevent the Irish from hiding in them during the rebellion.

I shall have to watch my beloved ships rotting on the strand, as I once saw the O'Flaherty ships.

When I was a child I went hunting with my father. I remember Dubhdara's hounds catching hares. When the hares felt the jaws closing down on them it seemed that there was nothing they could do.

But there must be something we can do, Toby. There must be.

Always,
Granuaile

chapter thirty-four
escape!

Hugh Dubh O'Donnell, earl of Tyrconnell, is in failing health. The old man knows he will not live to see an Ulster victory over the English. But Red Hugh might, leading the warriors of Tyrconnell. For that the young prince must be free.

O'Donnell seeks help from the earl of Tyrone. On behalf of his fellow chieftain, Hugh O'Neill writes urgent letters to people in London whom he can trust.

Bribes are quietly and skilfully arranged.

On Christmas night, 1591, the supposedly trustworthy men guarding Red Hugh O'Donnell remove his shackles. Then Red Hugh and two companions are allowed to walk unobserved in the yard of Dublin Castle. They promptly clamber up a wall, slide down a drainpipe on the outside and flee.

Their escape route lies across the Wicklow Mountains, where help has been arranged for them with one of the local chieftains. The weather is bitterly cold and the rain is bucketing down. One of the lads becomes separated from the others in the darkness. A second dies of cold and weakness before they can be rescued. But Red Hugh is soon on his way home to his father.

When he arrives, The O'Donnell resigns the leadership of the clan in his son's favour.

Granuaile is exultant. 'With a vigorous new chieftain to lead them, the men of Tyrconnell will join with Tyrone and defeat Elizabeth's forces!' she joyfully predicts.

❁   ❁   ❁

Unfortunately, Red Hugh's long imprisonment has damaged his health. It will be many months before he can take an active part in any uprising. He writes to the Spanish nobility, urging their aid for the Irish cause. He points out the ties of trade and religion between the two countries. The Armada is lost, he writes, but Spain and Ireland can still unite against the common enemy of England.

While rebellion simmers below the surface, Granuaile's personal horizon seems to be shrinking. Her ships lie abandoned. She has no herds. Her immense vitality is no use to her now. But she cannot give up. She has fought back so many times, and she must do so again. Yet how? How? What weapons has she to use against her arch-enemy, Richard Bingham?

Only her mind. Her clever, well educated mind.

❁   ❁   ❁

My dear Toby,

I need you to compose a petition in the English language, addressed to the queen. The document must not go through the lord deputy's hands. Fitzwilliam and Bingham are cut from the same piece of hide. I shall send the petition to my old friend, the duke of Ormond, and ask him to deliver it to Elizabeth in person. Black Thomas has become a favourite of hers, I understand.

In my petition, you are to describe me as Her Majesty's loyal and faithful subject, Grania O'Malley of Connacht.

Tell Elizabeth that I am an old woman, but one who is devoted to her. Explain that Richard Bingham has deliberately ruined both my ships and my livelihood. The property of my late husband, your father, has been taken from me. I retain only Rockfleet Castle, and I fear Bingham means to drive me out of this too. Ask Elizabeth to protect me from him. Further ask her to allow me a portion of Richard Bourke's property to maintain myself. Also beseech the queen to grant me the liberty to attack, with sword and fire, her enemies, wherever they shall be.

If she agrees to this she will have to give me my ships back.

Always,

Granuaile

chapter thirty-five

bingham strikes

The queen responds to Granuaile's petition with eighteen written questions. Elizabeth inquires about a wife's position under Gaelic law, and how much of her husband's property she is entitled to claim. The English queen also wants to know the personal details of Granuaile's life.

Through Tibbott, Granuaile replies. When describing her seafaring exploits she uses very guarded language. Naturally, she does not mention her plundering at all. Her answers are designed to arouse sympathy from Elizabeth Tudor, who has also spent a lifetime trying to outwit ambitious men. She orders that Granuaile's answers be put into the State Papers, and prepares to grant her requests.

Meanwhile Richard Bingham moves against Granuaile. He arrests both Tibbott and Granuaile's half-brother, Donal of the Pipes. They are charged with conspiring to murder Bingham. Witnesses are bribed to testify against them.

Granuaile is horrified. She had thought Tibbott, at least, was safe from Bingham. But the man has grown more vicious over the years. The time for written petitions is over – sending letters from Ireland to England takes too long. Only action will do now.

The tall she-king leans over a parapet at Rockfleet, gazing across the bay. She is very still, like the shimmering blue water. Yet beneath the surface her mind is busy. She is measuring her strength, her health, her energy. Weighing herself up against the task she proposes.

Her teeth clench. Her jaw thrusts forward and a light comes into her eyes. She whirls around and goes back into the tower, hurrying down the steep spiral stair almost as nimbly as a young girl. When she reaches the bottom she begins shouting for one of the few attendants who remain with her. 'I need someone who knows someone who has a horse!'

Granuaile summons help from old friends and acquaintances. They assemble enough material to make three galleys seaworthy. In late July, Granuaile sets sail for England … and the court of Elizabeth Tudor.

CHAPTER THIRTY-SIX

ELIZABETH

Although she will never admit it, Granuaile's heart is in her throat when she calls upon Elizabeth at her palace at Greenwich. The queen has already received angry letters from Bingham about her. It is up to Granuaile to present a very different picture of herself.

To remind Elizabeth that they are both she-kings, she dresses as a woman of the Gaelic nobility. The green velvet of her gown is fabric she herself once imported. The gown is made with slitted arms to reveal the bell-shaped sleeves of an Ulster linen smock beneath. The bodice is cut low to show that Granuaile's throat and bosom are still as firm as a girl's. Although they are the same age, Elizabeth cannot make the same boast.

Over her gown Granuaile wears a great fur cloak, lined with silk. Its fringed hem sweeps the ground. The English like to believe that the Irish go barefoot, but in truth, almost everyone has leather shoes. Until the English began seizing Irish herds there was plenty of leather.

For her meeting with Elizabeth, Granuaile selects a pair of soft boots made from Mayo hides. The toes are ornamented with gold embroidery.

Hidden in her belt is a dagger. A Spanish dagger.

The English never think to search this mere woman for weapons.

When Granuaile is brought before the queen in her audience chamber, she fights to hide her astonishment. She expected someone as tall as a Gaelic chieftain, a mighty monarch, a warrior like herself. But Elizabeth Tudor does not reach her shoulder. She is a wee brittle thing Granuaile could break over her knee.

Attendants cluster around the English queen, doing everything but breathe for her. Her face is as white as chalk. At first Granuaile thinks Elizabeth is ill. Then she realises the woman's skin is caked with powder.

Granuaile's heavy hair is pinned with silver bodkins. Elizabeth wears a red wig of a most unnatural hue. *Can it be the woman is bald?* Granuaile wonders.

The English queen's costume seems ridiculous. A vast lace collar surrounds her face and head. She cannot possibly see anyone sneaking up behind her. The bodice of her gown is so rigid she can hardly breathe. Jewels encrust her person from head to heels, weighing her down. Her feet are squeezed into tiny shoes with heels so high she can hardly walk. *What could she do if she was attacked?* Granuaile bites her lip to keep from laughing.

Then their eyes meet. And lock.

A strange sensation passes over Granuaile.

She knows Elizabeth. Knows her as she knows the sea or the wind. The queen of England is a woman who has suffered, as the Irish she-king has suffered. Granuaile feels a sudden pity for Elizabeth. This immensely powerful woman, imprisoned within her stiff clothes and her crowding courtiers, can never be free.

Granuaile refuses an interpreter and speaks with Elizabeth in Latin. The two women were born in the same year, Granuaile learns. 'Had we been born in the same place we might have been friends,' she says to the queen.

Elizabeth invites Granuaile to sit beside her while they talk together. Her courtiers wait, shifting from one foot to the other. The queen does not invite them to sit.

For all her physical weakness, it is soon obvious that Elizabeth Tudor has the mind of a born ruler. Hard, practical. Granuaile treats the queen with the respect she seeks for herself. She does not lie to Elizabeth. She does not tell all the truth, but what she does say is true.

She puts her case calmly and reasonably, and the queen listens in the same way. During the long afternoon they speak of many things. They discuss what it is like for a woman to be a leader of men. Elizabeth says she is amazed by Granuaile's success. Granuaile replies that she is equally amazed by Elizabeth.

The queen does not smile, but her eyes dance. They are fine eyes. She must have been beautiful, once.

When their meeting is over, Elizabeth offers Granuaile the hospitality of the palace until a decision is made about her case. Granuaile thanks her and starts to leave the chamber. Abruptly, the Irish woman sneezes. A great big whoop of a sneeze. The queen nods to one of her attendants, who hands Granuaile a tiny square of cambric.

She blows her nose long and loud. Then she tosses the handkerchief into the fire on the hearth.

Elizabeth cannot raise her eyebrows, for she has none. But there is icy disapproval in her voice. 'In England we put our used handkerchiefs back into our sleeves,' she says.

'In Ireland,' Granuaile replies, 'we are not so unclean that we stuff soiled handkerchiefs into our clothing.'

Elizabeth stares at her.

She stares back.

Slowly, Elizabeth begins to smile. The powder on her face cracks like glazed porcelain, but she smiles.

chapter thirty-seven

home in triumph

September, the Year of Our Lord 1593, Rockfleet

My dear Toby,

As you know by now, the queen of England has granted my petition in full. She has ordered that you and Donal be released, and further ordered that Richard Bingham cease his persecution of me. And, wonder of wonders! She has even given me permission to restore my fleet, so long as I use it to attack any who offend her.

My offer to use my ships on her behalf meant that it was in her best interest to return them to me.

When we set sail for home, I stood in the prow of my galley and gloried in the sweet wind on my face, blowing toward me from Ireland. The wind meant we could not use our sails, but my rowers bent to their task with a good will.

The most blessed journeys are always the ones you make going home.

I have just reached Rockfleet. By the time you receive this letter you will be at home at Burrishoole with your wife and your two little boys. Go to your chapel and give thanks.

And say a prayer for Elizabeth of England.

Always,

Granuaile

❋   ❋   ❋

By allowing Granuaile to restore her fleet, Elizabeth has given her permission to support herself in the old way. Bingham is furious, but there is nothing he can do.

Granuaile spends the winter at Rockfleet. She makes frequent journeys out to Clare Island to supervise the work being done on her galleys. Her overjoyed clansmen cluster around her, praising their she-king. Thanks to her, the sea is theirs again.

In spring the galleys take to the sea. They are rigged for fishing, but they do not fish. Once they are beyond observation they sail north to transport men and arms for O'Donnell and O'Neill.

The battle for Ireland continues.

By June of 1959, Red Hugh O'Donnell's men are pouring into Connacht. Many of the Bourkes are joining with them. Ulick Bourke attacks Sligo Castle and kills Toby's former host, George Bingham. 'If this causes you grief, I am sorry,' Granuaile tells her son. 'But the man was a Bingham, Toby.

'You would be well advised to join with O'Donnell and your Bourke kinsmen at this time,' Granuaile continues. 'The allies are planning their strategy carefully. This includes sending the queen a new petition. They shall ask her to have Richard Bingham tried for his failures as governor of Connacht. While I was at Greenwich I told the queen many things about Bingham, and she listened to me most carefully. One woman telling another of the wickedness and deceit of men.

'Elizabeth will blame Bingham for the bad policies that have brought the province to rebellion. If she gets rid of him for us altogether, it will be a great victory.'

In the great hall at Rockfleet, Granuaile props her feet on a stool and leans back with a contented sigh. Shaggy hounds lie at her feet. A fire roars in the hearth.

In her fingers is a letter.

Richard Bingham has been ordered to stand trial in Athlone. Fearful of the outcome, he has fled to England. There he was seized by Elizabeth's men and promptly imprisoned.

The duke of Ormond has written his old friend, Granuaile, with the news.

'I hope Bingham's cell is full of rats,' she murmurs to the hounds.

chapter thirty-eight

turning against o'donnell

December, the Year of Our Lord 1595, Rockfleet

My dear Toby,

Now that Shane MacOliverus's brother is dead and the title is vacant again, I was furious to learn that O'Donnell is not supporting you for the MacWilliamship. When his army marched into Mayo and drove back the English, it seemed like an answer to our prayers. I was happy enough to see him take control of the region. I never thought he would prefer someone else as chieftain of the Mayo Bourkes. It is a dreadful mistake. He forgets what a good ally I have been to the princes of the north.

Many of your father's kinsmen will turn against O'Donnell because of this. I shall see to it. Red Hugh and I have long been friends, or so I thought. But now he has acted against my son's interest.

Who are our true friends? Whom can we really rely upon? When I look back at my youth everything seemed so clear. I do not know any more.

Perhaps I am just growing old, Toby. When I count up my years, I find that I have endured sixty-six winters. Yet I do not feel old inside myself. When I first awake in the morning I am the same woman I always was. I jump up from my bed, eager for the day. Then my bones creak and my muscles ache and I am reminded.

I wonder if Elizabeth feels the same.

Even age has lessons to teach us. It is not possible to live in the past, and today will be over too soon. Prepare for the future, my son.

Always,

Granuaile

◈ ◈ ◈

The ravenous armies from Donegal are reducing Mayo to near famine.

Granuaile encourages the Bourkes to desert Red Hugh O'Donnell.

Furious, he turns his men loose to plunder her lands. Her rebuilt herd is slaughtered. Then O'Donnell's warriors march to Toby's stronghold at Burrishoole and cause the same damage there.

Early in 1597 a new governor, Sir Clifford Conyers, is appointed for Connacht. He immediately moves against O'Donnell. When the Bourkes will not stand with the Donegal chieftain, Conyers succeeds in driving him back into Ulster.

chapter thirty-nine

the wind has changed

April, the Year of Our Lord 1597, Clare Island

My dear Toby,

I have come to a most difficult decision. There is no longer enough strength in me to captain my ships. This morning I slipped and fell on deck. I could not get up on my own. My men had to help me up, and then they carried me here to the tower house. I burn with shame, Toby. Never again will I allow that to happen.

I have decided to turn over my ships and men to you.

You need not captain the fleet yourself. You can appoint any of half a dozen experienced men from among my crews. Both O'Malleys and O'Flaherties know the trade routes. You should do especially well with wool and linen next year. But do not squander your profits. Use them as I tell you.

Your foster-father, Myles MacEvilly, is very old and ill. The income from the fleet will enable you to purchase his holdings when he dies. Arrange the purchase according to English law. That way you can be sure of keeping your property.

Kings – and she-kings – come and go, but the land endures.

Always,
Granuaile

◉   ◉   ◉

Giving up her fleet is the hardest thing Granuaile has ever done. It hurts like a knife wound to the chest. After she writes the letter she leaves it lying on the table. Beside it are her favourite Italian pistol and her pewter tankard, half-full of red wine. The pistol, as always, is loaded. The wine is from the last casks she will ever import.

She wanders around the chamber. Pauses beside the hearth to poke up the fire. Rubs an aching hip. Leans into an embrasure to gaze out of the narrow window.

Clew Bay is dark and still. After a few minutes, a run of ripples sweeps across the water toward Rockfleet.

Granuaile nods. 'You are a foolish old woman,' she chuckles. 'Can you not see the wind has changed?' Striding to the table, she drains the tankard in one long swallow. Then she shouts for a messenger. 'Here is a letter for my son at Burrishoole. Send a galley across the bay at once.'

After he leaves, she throws back her head and draws herself up until she is standing straight and proud. 'So on we go!'

epilogue

May, the Year of Our Lord 1603, Rockfleet

My dear son Myles,

I have sad news. Although I rode hard when I left Burrishoole, I reached Rockfleet too late to bid your grandmother goodbye. I shall remain here to arrange for her entombment on Clare Island.

There are many things I wish I had said to her while there was still time. Somehow I never thought she would die. Like Elizabeth Tudor, Granuaile seemed immortal. Perhaps she is in a way. You have her dark hair and eyes. Your brother Theobald has her laugh.

Your grandmother was a remarkable woman. People thought her wild and reckless, and she was. Yet she was clever and thoughtful too. These are the gifts she passed on to me.

In 1601, when O'Neill and O'Donnell marched south to fight the English at Kinsale, I know her heart went with them. Although she had quarrelled with Red Hugh O'Donnell, they were fighting for Gaelic Ireland, the cause which Granuaile had championed all her life.

My mother urged me to take men to the field myself. I did, but I waited until the last moment to decide how best to use my small army. When I saw that we could not hope to win, I threw in my lot with Mountjoy and the English.

When I returned to Mayo I was almost afraid to face my mother. But she surprised me. She said, 'You are on the winning side now, so take advantage of the opportunity. Build a secure future for yourself and for your sons. Life and land are what matter, Toby. Life and land.'

Do you remember the messenger who arrived just as I was leaving Burrishoole? He trotted beside my horse, shouting his news to me as I rode away. Hugh O'Neill, Earl of Tyrone, has surrendered to the Crown. The war to preserve Gaelic Ireland is over.

Elizabeth's men did not tell O'Neill the queen was dead until after he had signed the document.

The she-king of Mayo and the she-king of England have died in the same year.

The messenger gave me more news. England has a new king now. He is James, son of Mary of Scotland. James intends to grant me a knighthood for my services at Kinsale. I shall become Sir Tibbott Bourke of Mayo.

I wonder what Granuaile would have said. Would she have laughed?

Always,

Toby